Elizabeth Gail
and the dangerous double

Hilda Stahl

WindRider BOOKS
Tyndale House Publishers, Inc., Wheaton, Illinois

Dedicated with love to
Gary, Dottie, Bret, and Aaron Clements

The Elizabeth Gail Series

Tenth printing, October 1987

Library of Congress Catalog Card Number 79-55754
ISBN 0-8423-0723-0, paper
Copyright © 1980 by Hilda Stahl.
All rights reserved.
Printed in the United States of America.

Contents

One
Toby Johnson

Libby wildly searched the yard for a place to hide before she burst into tears in front of everyone. Her heart almost stopped as Brenda Wilkens walked toward her. Brenda was dressed as if she was going to church instead of an outdoor open house in Toby's honor.

Libby rubbed her hands down her jeans and looked frantically for a way to dodge Brenda. Where was Ben? He'd promised to keep Brenda from making trouble.

Libby slipped behind Connie Tol, who was asking Toby how he liked being adopted into the Johnson family. Libby blinked hard to keep the tears back as Toby answered excitedly. Of course he was glad! Who wouldn't be?

Goosy Poosy honked indignantly from the chicken pen where Kevin had locked him until after Toby's special party. Libby looked at Goosy Poosy and shivered. Maybe she should turn him

loose to fly against Brenda and knock her down.
She wouldn't look so smug then.

Rex barked, tugging at the chain to which
Libby had tied him earlier. Vera had said that
Rex couldn't run loose with all the guests
around. He might jump up on someone in his
excitement.

Libby knelt beside him and hugged him with
her face pressed against his black and tan hair.
"Oh, Rex! Toby's adopted. And I want to be! It's
not fair! It's not!"

Rex whined and wriggled. He tried to lick
Libby's face.

Was everyone looking at her and wondering
why the Johnsons hadn't adopted her? Did they
feel sorry for her? Maybe they were glad Toby
was adopted and she wasn't. Everyone had
brought gifts for Toby. He'd stood by the table
with Chuck and Vera beside him and opened
everything. He hadn't sucked his thumb once.
With his hair as red as Chuck's, they could pass
for real father and son. Vera had kissed him and
acted as if he were her real son.

Libby touched her hair. It was brown and ugly
and didn't look like anyone else's in the Johnson
family. She wouldn't pass for one of the family at
all. She was tall and skinny and ugly. Nobody
would kiss her in front of all those people and say
she was her real daughter. Susan, Kevin, and
Ben were the real Johnson kids. Toby was an
adopted Johnson, but she was still a foster girl, an

aid kid who didn't really belong anywhere.

Libby looked at Grandma and Grandpa Johnson as they sat beside the table of food. They'd driven a long way to be here on Toby's special day. Libby watched as Grandpa called Toby to him and slipped his arm around him.

Libby looked quickly away and caught sight of Brenda pushing her way toward her. Quickly Libby slipped around the dog house toward the side of the house. She couldn't let Brenda catch her. Oh, where was Ben? He said he would help keep Brenda away.

Susan called to Libby and motioned for her to join her. Libby shook her head sharply. She couldn't talk with Susan and her friends right now. They would be sure to say something about Toby being in the family now and how wonderful it must be.

If only she could get to the side door and sneak inside where Brenda couldn't find her! Then she could hide in her room with Pinky, the big pink dog Susan had given her when she'd first moved in with the Johnsons, and with Teddy, the teddy bear that Grandma Feuder and Bob Dupont had given her for helping them. Pinky and Teddy wouldn't make fun of her and call her aid kid.

Just as Libby reached the door, someone grabbed her arm. She glared over her shoulder, expecting to see Brenda, then sighed in relief. "Hi, Joe." He was Brenda's brother but he was never mean. He was her friend.

"Come play ball with us, Elizabeth."

She liked him to call her Elizabeth. For just a minute she felt better.

"We're going to play in back of the chicken house. Ben and some of the boys are fixing a ball diamond now." Joe slapped his mitt against his leg. "Susan and some of the other girls are going to play."

"Brenda too?" asked Libby sharply.

Joe laughed, shaking his dark head. "You know she wouldn't play. She might get messed up a little. But she told Ben she'd watch him."

And Libby knew she would. Brenda would get mad if another girl even looked at Ben. Libby remembered all the mean things Brenda had done to her out of jealousy. Libby took a deep breath. "I don't want to play ball today, Joe."

"But you're the best batter. I wanted you on my team."

Libby smiled. She wasn't *that* good. Joe was just trying to make her feel better. "I guess I can play for a while."

Just then Dave Boomer called Joe and he ran off, yelling over his shoulder that he'd see Libby in the field. She watched him run, his long legs flying. Joe could run almost as fast as Ben.

Libby walked around the crowd of people. Goosy Poosy honked as she hurried past the chicken pen. "You're too noisy," said Libby, playfully shaking her finger at the big white goose. "Kevin will let you out later."

"I should let him out now."

Libby spun around and gasped as Brenda stopped beside the chicken pen gate. "Don't you dare open that! You'll be in big trouble if you do."

Brenda threw her head back and laughed, her long, dark hair flowing down her slender back. "I'd just tell everyone that you did it."

"No one would believe you," said Libby, her heart racing. But someone might. Brenda could tell a lie to make it sound like the truth.

"Why aren't you standing with Toby around all the happy people?" asked Brenda with a wicked twinkle in her dark eye. "Toby *Johnson* is a very happy boy today. Are you happy, aid kid?"

Libby knotted her fists at her side. How she wanted to punch Brenda! But she wouldn't do it. She'd promised Jesus that he could be in charge of her life. Jesus wanted her to love Brenda Wilkens. And that seemed impossible!

"Do you know why you aren't the one being adopted instead of Toby?" Brenda shoved her face close to Libby's. "Nobody wants you, that's why. You're Elizabeth Gail Dobbs and that's who you're always going to be!"

Libby took a deep breath, forcing down the bitter taste in her mouth. She turned away from Brenda, but Brenda grabbed her arm and spun her around.

"You're really jealous that Toby is adopted and you aren't. And you're never going to be! You're an aid kid and you'll always be an aid kid!"

Libby's fist shot out and caught Brenda on the

nose. Blood spurted. Brenda screamed. Libby raced away, her ears ringing. Brenda was right! She was only an aid kid. She'd always be an aid kid.

Libby dropped to the ground behind a tall oak and sobbed against the cool grass. She was Elizabeth Gail Dobbs. She'd never be Elizabeth Gail Johnson! "Dobb the Slob." That's what Brenda often called her, and that's just what she was!

Two
Love

Strong arms lifted Libby from the ground. She blinked and sniffed as she looked into Chuck Johnson's face. She tried to pull away before he could scold her, but he held her firmly.

"Elizabeth, just stand quietly and tell me what's wrong." Gently he wiped tears from her face with his white hanky.

She pressed her forehead against his chest. "Oh, Dad! I hit Brenda Wilkens! I'm so sorry!" She wanted to tell him that she was a nothing. She wanted to ask if he would adopt her if he could. But the words were locked tightly inside. It would hurt too much to say them aloud. It would hurt too much to hear the answer.

Chuck stroked her hair as he held her. She stood almost as tall as he. It felt good to be held and patted and soothed, Libby thought. She wanted to stay there forever. Finally he held her away and looked down into her face.

"Why did you hit Brenda? I know you

wouldn't do it just for the fun of it. What did Brenda do to you?"

Libby sniffed. Her throat ached from crying. She saw tear stains on Chuck's light blue jacket. "She . . . she called me an aid kid," whispered Libby.

"But she always calls you that." Chuck brushed grass off Libby's yellow jacket. "Jesus has been helping you to forgive and to love Brenda. What aren't you telling me?"

Libby's heart raced. She swallowed hard. "She . . . she was teasing me because Toby's adopted and I'm not." Libby kept her eyes glued to the toes of her white and blue tennis shoes. What would Chuck say now?

He took her hand in his and squeezed it. "Elizabeth, I love you. Mom and the kids love you. It took Toby a while, but he loves you, too." He gently lifted her face so she'd look at him. "If your mother would sign the papers, we'd adopt you. You belong to us, honey. A different last name doesn't keep us from loving you and thinking of you as our daughter."

Libby flung her arms around Chuck's neck and hugged him tightly. "Oh, Dad! I love you! I'm so glad you'd adopt me if you could!" She wanted to shout and laugh and leap around the field. They loved her! Chuck loved her!

Chuck laughed. "That's quite a bear hug. It's a good thing you aren't stronger or you'd have choked me."

14

Libby giggled and dropped her arms. Her hazel eyes sparkled and she felt warm all over.

Chuck slipped his arm around her shoulders and slowly walked toward the house. "Mom took Brenda into the house and took care of her bloody nose. I'm sure she'll be all right. But Elizabeth, I think you have something to take care of, don't you?"

Libby's stomach knotted. "Do I have to tell her I'm sorry?"

Chuck was quiet a long time. "We're all learning to do what God's Word tells us to do. What is Jesus' command to us?"

Libby licked her dry lips. She wanted to pull away from Chuck and run. She whispered, "That we love."

"And we love others no matter how they treat us. You can't love Brenda Wilkens by yourself. But Jesus can put his love for Brenda into you, then you'll be able to love and forgive Brenda. And then you can apologize to her and mean it."

Libby sighed. She didn't want to love or forgive Brenda. But Libby knew that she couldn't go by what she felt. Dad had said just yesterday that when you obey the Word, even when you don't feel like it, the "feeling like it" would come after the obeying. Silently Libby asked Jesus to give her love for Brenda. Libby looked up at Chuck. "I'll see if Brenda's still in the house. I'll tell her that I'm sorry."

"That's my girl." Chuck kissed the tip of her

nose. "After that come to the pen beside the horse barn and we'll give Toby a ride on his new pony."

Libby smiled and nodded. Toby had been very excited when Dad had led the pony from the barn and said it was his. He hadn't had a chance to ride him yet. Libby remembered the first time she'd climbed on Ben's horse. It had seemed to be a mile off the ground. Ben had been so patient with her as she learned to ride. Toby would have fun learning on his pony.

Libby stopped outside the back door of the house and took a deep breath. She knew Jesus would help her talk to Brenda.

Slowly Libby walked in. She heard voices coming from the kitchen. Her heart raced as she walked into the kitchen. Brenda sat at the kitchen table and Vera stood beside the sink.

Vera smiled. "We've been waiting for you, Libby."

Libby locked her fingers together. She looked right at Brenda. "I'm sorry for hitting you. I'd like you to forgive me." Libby even managed a smile.

Brenda jumped up, glaring angrily at Libby. "I hate you! I'll never, never forgive you. You probably broke my nose! And my blouse is ruined!"

"No it isn't, Brenda," said Vera firmly. "Your nose is fine and the blood will easily wash out of that blouse if you use cold water."

16

Brenda knotted her fists. "I'm leaving! And you can't make me stay here any longer."

"You're welcome to go now that Libby has had a chance to talk to you," said Vera. She slid an arm around Libby's waist and pulled her close to her side. "You really should go home right away and wash that blouse, Brenda. I'll tell your parents all about it."

Brenda's face flushed red, then paled. "They don't need to know about it. I can wash my blouse myself." She dashed from the room. The outside door slammed behind her.

Libby looked up at Vera. "I'm sorry, Mom, for causing trouble for you." Mom smelled like a flower. She looked pretty with her shoulder-length blonde hair and light green pantsuit.

Vera hugged Libby close. "I'm glad that you apologized to Brenda. I'm sure Brenda had that punch in the nose coming to her, but it would've been better for you if you'd just ignored her. She is a very unhappy girl, and for some reason she takes it out on you."

Quietly Libby explained to Vera what had happened with Brenda, then what Chuck had said.

Vera kissed Libby on both cheeks, then held her close for a while. She had tears in her eyes as she held Libby away from her. "I love you, honey. You are as precious to me as Susan, as the boys. Someday your mother will sign the papers so we can adopt you. In the meantime, you're still ours."

Libby smiled. "I won't ever have to go live with Mother again, will I?"

Vera hesitated and Libby shivered.

"I won't, will I, Mom?" Libby asked frantically.

"I don't think so, Libby. Miss Miller said that as long as she's your caseworker, she'll never allow you to be given back to your mother. Miss Miller knows how many times you were left in foster home after foster home when your mother deserted you all those times. Miss Miller will see that you stay right here with us where you belong. We prayed you here, and here you'll stay!"

"And I'm glad! I won't ever even get married. I'll live here with you all my life."

Vera laughed. "You say that now when you're twelve years old. But what about when you're twenty and some young man comes along."

"That'll never happen to me!" Libby couldn't picture herself grown up. "Then I'll get married and we'll live here."

Vera laughed again. "I think we'd better get back outdoors. Dad said he was going to saddle Toby's pony and give him a ride. Grandpa's going to take pictures."

Libby walked outdoors with Vera. The sun was lower in the sky and left a chill behind. Libby shivered. "I'm going to put my warm jacket on," she said. "I'll be right back."

As she ran back to the house, she hummed happily. It was a song that she'd been practicing on the piano. Someday she wanted to play as well as Vera. Someday she wanted to be a concert pianist.

Just as she reached for the doorknob, Joe called to her. Did he know that she'd given his sister a bloody nose? Would he be mad?

Joe just smiled, then looked down as if he was embarrassed about something. "I'm sorry about Brenda causing trouble for you. I told Mom and Dad about it and they went home with her. Dad said she can't come back today. If you want me to go home, I will." His dark eyes were sad as he looked at her.

Libby shook her head. "You're my friend, Joe. Stay as long as you want. I don't blame you for what Brenda did to me. And I am sorry for hitting Brenda. I won't do it again."

Joe doubled his fist. "But I might!"

"No! Don't, Joe. Besides, it's hard to say you're sorry afterward." Libby laughed and finally Joe did too. Libby opened the back door. "I want to get another jacket. Wait for me and we'll go watch Toby ride his pony."

Joe followed her in. As she hung up her yellow jacket he said, "I have something for you, Elizabeth."

She turned in surprise. "You do?"

"Everyone brought gifts to Toby today." Joe pulled a small box from his pocket. "I got something for you."

Libby wanted to hug him, but she took the box and stared at it, just enjoying the fact that he'd thought about her. "What is it?" she asked breathlessly.

He laughed. "Open it and see." He stuffed his hands in his pockets and hunched his thin shoulders. "I hope you like it."

Slowly she lifted the lid and looked inside the box. "Oh, Joe! Oh, Joe!" It was a miniature grand piano for her to set on her desk. She touched the tiny keys and legs. Tears sparkled in her eyes. Joe knew how much she loved the piano. She looked at him, then finally said, "Thank you very much. I love it."

Joe grinned. "I guess we'd better get outdoors or we won't see Toby riding his pony."

"I guess we'd better." Libby slipped the box into her jacket pocket. She'd keep her gift right where she could touch it often.

They hurried outdoors toward the crowd of people clustered around the horse pen.

Three
The invitation

Libby smiled as Toby rode around and around the pen on Dusty, his very own pony. Libby knew how excited and happy Toby was to have a pony of his own. Dusty was already friends with Sleepy, Kevin's pony.

Joe crawled through the fence to stand with Ben. Miss Miller walked over to Libby.

"This is a wonderful day for Toby," said Miss Miller with a warm smile. She was dressed in a cranberry red pantsuit and a flowered blouse. Today her hair was loose around her face instead of pinned back. Libby thought she looked very pretty. Once Libby had hated her and thought she was ugly and mean. "Toby is very happy."

Libby agreed. She was glad Miss Miller had found the time to come for Toby's special day. Miss Miller was always very busy and seemed rushed. She took care of lots of foster children, finding them homes and seeing that they were happy and well adjusted.

Miss Miller sighed. "Not many of my boys and girls have happy endings. But you and Toby do, Libby, and I'm pleased."

Libby leaned close so only Miss Miller could hear her. "Why can't you get Mother to sign the papers so I can be adopted?"

"I wish I could, Libby. So far she's refused to sign. But we won't give up. When she gets back from Australia, I'll contact her in person."

Weakly Libby leaned against the fence. "Is she coming back?"

"You knew she would, Libby. She might already be back. She'll contact me when she's ready. She always does." Miss Miller's voice was tight and angry. It made Libby shiver. Then Miss Miller smiled and the scared feeling left Libby. "As long as I'm your caseworker, Libby, you won't have to worry about your mother. I know how destructive she is and I will not allow her to take you from the Johnsons." Miss Miller patted Libby's thin shoulder. "I'll keep trying to get her to sign the paper allowing you to be adopted."

"Thank you," whispered Libby. She almost believed the day would come. And if it did, she'd have a party just like Toby's and invite everyone so they knew she was really a Johnson.

"I'm going on vacation next week," said Miss Miller. "I'll only be gone two weeks, so I'm sure you won't need me for anything."

"Are you going to Florida?" Libby's Sunday school teacher Connie Tol had just gotten back from Florida. She was tanned a pretty brown and had said it was so warm she'd wanted to stay until summer.

"No. I'm only going a few miles up north." Miss Miller looked dreamy and far away. "I want to go to the town where I grew up. I want to try to find someone."

Just then Grandpa called Libby. He stood inside the pen with his big camera. "I want you to stand beside Toby on his pony so I can take your picture," said Grandpa.

Libby hesitated. She didn't want her picture taken.

"Come on, Libby," said Susan, motioning to her. "Stand beside me."

Libby reluctantly ran to Susan. Susan looked small and pretty. Libby felt tall and skinny and ugly. Susan's hair was long and red-gold. She had it in two ponytails that bobbed as she talked. Libby touched her own plain hair.

Finally Grandpa stopped clicking pictures. He handed the camera to Grandma, then walked to Libby.

"I haven't seen much of you today, Elizabeth," he said with a grin. He was taller and leaner than Chuck, and his red hair had a lot of gray in it. He jingled the change in his pocket. "How about going for a walk with me?"

"Sure," she said happily. She liked talking to Grandpa. "Do you want to see the new calves?"

"I'd like to very much." Grandpa opened the gate, let Libby walk through, and then closed it. "Have you been doctoring any more animals?"

23

Libby giggled. The family always let her take care of sick animals. They said she had a way with animals. "I've had to bucket-feed one of the calves. I named her Princess. She walks around like a real princess."

They talked as they walked to the cow barn. It was cooler inside than out. Libby was glad she had on her warmer jacket. She showed Grandpa the new calves. A barn cat mewed and rubbed against Libby's leg. She picked it up and held it close. It smelled like old milk and dust.

Grandpa scratched the cat on the head, his blue eyes sparkling happily. He teased Libby about her animal family. Libby liked to have him tease her. She knew he did it because he loved her.

Several cars were driving out of the driveway as Libby walked with Grandpa back to the house. She fingered the box from Joe which was in her pocket. Her day was turning out to be great.

"Let's go sit with Grandma," said Grandpa. "She looks tired. I'd better get her inside and fix her a cup of hot tea. Your grandma likes hot tea. I could use a cup too. With the sun almost down, it's turned quite cold."

"Libby girl, sit down and talk to me," said Grandma with a tired smile. "I haven't had a chance to talk to you all day."

"We're going to take you inside and make you a cup of tea," said Libby, smiling. "Grandpa wants one too."

24

Grandma pushed herself up with a groan. "What a day! I'm glad we aren't driving back until tomorrow." She slipped her hand through Grandpa's arm. "Have you told her?"

"Not yet."

Libby looked from one to the other. Did they mean *her*? Was the news good? Or would it make her feel bad?

"We have a surprise for you, Libby," said Grandma. "But I want to wait and tell you after I have that hot cup of tea."

Libby squirmed impatiently. She couldn't wait to hear. It seemed to take forever for the teakettle to boil. She handed Grandma the sugar bowl. Didn't they know she couldn't wait to hear what the surprise was?

Finally she sat at the kitchen table with them. She held a glass of orange juice. She tried to sip it, but it wouldn't go down. Wouldn't they ever tell her?

Grandpa sat his cup down. "Elizabeth, next week is your spring vacation from school. We want you to come visit us for the next two weeks. Your dad got permission from your teachers for you to miss a week of school. Would you like to come stay with us for two weeks?"

Libby blinked, her heart racing.

"We really want you, Libby," said Grandma softly. "We want a chance to have you to ourselves for a while."

Libby shivered excitedly. She'd always wanted to visit grandparents like other kids did. It would

25

be fun to pack her clothes. She would be just like other kids. How exciting it would be to tell everyone that she was going away for two weeks to stay with her grandparents!

"Speak to us, Libby," said Grandma with a worried frown. "Is something wrong?"

"You don't have to come if you don't want to," said Grandpa, fingering his tea cup.

Libby gasped. "Oh, I want to come! It's the best thing in the world! Did Mom and Dad really say I could go?"

Grandpa laughed and took her hand, holding it firmly. "It's all planned. You'll ride the bus to our house and then we'll bring you home."

Grandma leaned across the table toward Libby. "You might not enjoy it as much as you seem to think. We live in a tiny town and we don't know any kids your age. You might get bored."

Libby jumped up and ran around to hug Grandma. "I won't get bored. I want to visit you. Oh, wow! A surprise visit! The best surprise I ever had!" She looked up as Chuck and Vera walked in.

"I see you like the surprise," said Chuck as he pulled out a chair and sat down. "There is just a slight change."

Libby held her breath.

Vera sat down and reached for Libby's hand. "Miss Miller is going on vacation and will drive right past Alton. She said she'd be glad for your company. We'll feel better if you ride with her instead of taking a bus."

"That sounds wonderful," said Grandpa. "Don't you agree, Elizabeth?"

Libby laughed in relief. "It will be super! I can't wait until it's time to go."

"Hey, don't be too anxious," said Chuck with a laugh. "You sound as if you can't wait to get away."

"Oh, no, Dad. But I can't wait to visit Grandma and Grandpa just like a normal girl. I have a family, a real family with parents, grandparents, and brothers and a sister." Her day had started out terrible but had turned into one of the best days of her life!

Four
Miss Miller

Libby squirmed to try to find a more comfortable position. She looked at Miss Miller. She didn't seem to mind the long hours of sitting still. They had long since passed the heavy traffic of the large city and were driving through quiet countryside. The sun shone warmly through Libby's window.

"How much longer?" asked Libby.

"About an hour." Miss Miller rubbed her hand across her eyes. "I'm beginning to get tired, too. Would you like me to put on some music? I have a few cassettes of good music."

Libby shrugged. She could smell Miss Miller's nice perfume and it reminded her of the time Miss Miller had taken her to the Johnson farm to live. "You do know the way to Grandpa's, don't you?"

"Of course. I've been through Alton several times. Paxton is only ten miles or so from there."

Miss Miller sighed. "It's been a long time since I've been there."

"Does your family live there?" Libby twisted in her seat so she could watch Miss Miller's expressive face.

"No. I just wanted to see if I could look up old friends. All my girl friends are married with families."

"Did you want to get married?" Libby saw the sad look on Miss Miller's face and she wished she hadn't asked.

"Once I did very much. But he married someone else." Miss Miller blinked. "If I had married, I'd have never met you, Libby. I'm satisfied with my life. Maybe someday I'll fall in love again."

It felt strange to have Miss Miller talk to her that way.

"I'm happy the way your life has changed," continued Miss Miller. "You are certainly different from the girl that I first met a few years ago. The Johnsons have been very good for you." Miss Miller brushed her hair away from her face. She smiled at Libby, then looked back at the road. "I know the biggest change came from taking Jesus as your personal Savior. I can say that was the greatest change in my life, too. I've been a Christian about two years now. And I wouldn't want it any different."

Libby rubbed her hands down her jeans. Miss Miller had never, ever talked to her about anything except her case. But it did kind of feel good—as though Miss Miller considered her a friend, not just another case history.

Suddenly the car coughed and sputtered. Libby leaned forward, her hands clenched in her lap. What was wrong?

"Oh, dear," said Miss Miller with a worried frown. "What is the matter with my car?" She pulled to the edge of the road but the car stopped the strange noises, and so she drove back onto the road. "I think we'd better keep going. I wouldn't want to hunt down a farmer to ask for help."

Libby didn't feel very worried. Dad had told her that God was with them, protecting them, and that he would always be with them. Libby knew that God answered prayer. He'd answered many prayers for her, and he would take care of them now.

"If we can make it to Alton, maybe your grandpa will know what's wrong," said Miss Miller. "This hasn't happened before." She nervously brushed her hand across her eyes. "I should've taken 'powder puff' mechanics."

"Don't worry, Miss Miller. Dad said we have angels watching over us. We'll get to Grandpa's safe. You'll see." Libby smiled. She could see Miss Miller relax.

"I am learning to trust completely in God," she said. "Sometimes I forget that he loves me enough to know right where I am at all times. We will make it to your grandpa's house."

The car sputtered and coughed two more

times before they drove into Alton and down the quiet main street to Nash Street.

"There's the house," cried Libby excitedly as she pointed at a big white house with a tan roof and shutters. "See! There's Grandpa's car!"

Miss Miller pulled into the drive and shut off the engine. She leaned back and looked at Libby with a glad smile. "We made it! Thank God!"

Libby scrambled out of the car just as the front door opened and her grandparents rushed out. Grandma hugged her close. She smelled like fresh baked cookies, Libby thought. Libby hugged Grandpa next as Grandma greeted Miss Miller.

"It's good to see you, Elizabeth. I was beginning to think you wouldn't get here this morning. It's almost lunchtime. Grandma fixed a delicious lunch for all of us." He turned to Miss Miller. "We would love to have you stay for lunch. We've planned on it."

"You need a little rest after all that driving, dear," said Grandma.

Miss Miller smiled. "I'd like to stay. Thanks. Maybe after lunch you could check over my car." She described the noises and Grandpa offered to look it over.

Libby's stomach growled with hunger as they unloaded her suitcase. She couldn't wait to eat. Maybe Grandma had baked cookies especially for her. Libby carried in her new gray purse that Susan had given her for the trip. Inside her purse was the tiny piano that Joe had given her. She

31

just had to bring it. When she'd said goodbye to Joe he'd looked very sad. He told her he'd miss her. Her family had said they'd miss her. Libby had felt strange. No one had ever missed her before when she'd left. No one had ever cared enough to miss her.

Lunch was tuna and egg salad sandwiches, carrot sticks, cottage cheese, apple sauce, milk to drink, and fresh baked chocolate chip cookies. Libby ate until she couldn't manage another bite.

Miss Miller leaned back in her chair with a satisfied sigh. "That was the most delicious lunch I've had in a long, long time. Thank you, Mrs. Johnson. I'm glad you invited me to stay."

"We were glad to have you. We thank you very much for bringing our Libby, Miss Miller," said Grandma.

"Oh, please, call me Gwen," said Miss Miller.

"Well, Gwen, let's take a look at that car of yours," said Grandpa, pushing back his chair and standing up.

Libby jumped up too. She wanted to poke her head under the hood with Grandpa. Maybe he could teach her a little mechanics. Libby smiled. She'd watched Dad and Ben working on Dad's pickup. Ben had always gotten very greasy. She didn't know if she'd want to get that messy.

Miss Miller slid behind the steering wheel and turned on the key. Nothing happened. She tried again. Still nothing.

Libby stood beside Grandpa and looked under

the hood. Everything looked strange to Libby. How could Grandpa look at all that stuff and know what was wrong?

"Is there a garage in town that would fix it?" asked Miss Miller as she walked around to stand beside Grandpa.

He jingled his keys in his pockets and frowned thoughtfully. "There is one mechanic in town, but he's gone for the day." Grandpa ran his fingers through his hair. "I think you'd better plan on spending the night with us, Gwen. We have plenty of room. Tomorrow we'll get your car running again and you can be on your way. Will that mess up your plans?"

Miss Miller sighed. "Not really. But I hate to put you folks out. I can stay in a motel."

"We don't have one. You just come in the house and make yourself at home with us. We'd love to have you, wouldn't we, Elizabeth?"

Libby nodded. "Please stay, Miss Miller. You can always leave tomorrow. And you can share my room if you want."

"No need for that," said Grandpa as he unlocked her trunk and lifted out her suitcases. "We have another bedroom all ready."

Grandma came out and added her argument to the others, and finally Miss Miller agreed.

It didn't take long for Libby to settle in her room. She put the piano from Joe on the dresser next to her brush and comb. She touched it and thought about Joe.

Several minutes later Miss Miller poked her

head in the door. "How about going for a walk with me? Are you too tired?"

"Oh, no! I'd like to go for a walk." She slipped on her green sweater that made her eyes look green. "I saw a park when we drove through town. Can we walk to it?"

"I'd like that," said Miss Miller, zipping up her plaid jacket. "In fact I'd like to swing on an old-fashioned rope swing like I saw there." She tapped Libby playfully on the nose. "You are going to think I'm strange if I don't watch out."

Libby laughed. She liked it when Miss Miller acted this way. She didn't seem so old or businesslike.

Slowly they walked down the sidewalk. Loud music drifted out of a brown house. A baby cried inside a small white house. Were all the children in school? Maybe they had spring vacation later in the month. Or maybe they'd already had it.

Libby walked around a tricycle. A bee buzzed past her head, then landed on a rose bush that was leafed out. Soon it would be full of roses.

A woman walked across the street just ahead of them. Libby gasped and clutched Miss Miller's arm.

"Look," she whispered through dry lips. The woman had bleached blonde hair. She was tall and slender and dressed in a tight yellow skirt and sweater.

Miss Miller stopped. "Oh, Libby!"

"It's Mother," whispered Libby in agony. "It's Mother, back from Australia."

34

Five
New relatives

Libby didn't want to wake up. She knew there was something terrible to remember if she did. A noise beside her bed startled her. She gasped in surprise. A little boy about four years old stood beside her bed just looking at her. He had wide blue eyes and red-gold hair like Susan's. Libby cleared her throat. "Who are you?" she asked as she pushed herself to her elbows. She knew her hair was in tangles and that her eyes had dark circles under them. She'd tossed and turned for a long time last night. Mother was in town!

The little boy leaned against the bed. "I'm Scottie Johnson. Are you Lizbeth?"

Libby managed a smile. "Call me Libby. It's easier to say."

He grinned. "Will you play with me, Libby? Pop bought me a new truck and Grandpa bought me a tractor like Uncle Chuck's."

Libby gasped in surprise as she swung out of

35

bed. Her nightgown brushed the rust-colored carpet. This boy Scottie was related to the Johnsons that she lived with. But how? She hadn't heard about anyone except Grandma and Grandpa Johnson. Did Scottie live with them?

Just then Grandma stuck her head into Libby's room. She had on a pink flowered dress and a pink apron. She smiled. "I see you and Scottie are getting acquainted, Libby. I hope he didn't wake you."

"I didn't know you had anyone living with you." Libby sank to the edge of the bed. Her legs had seemed to turn to rubber when she'd seen Mother, and they still didn't seem strong.

Grandma rested her hand on Scottie's head. "This is our son Luke's boy. His name is Scott Russell Johnson."

"I'm named after Grandpa," said Scottie proudly. "His name is Russell."

Libby couldn't remember anyone ever talking about Luke or Scottie. Maybe they had and she hadn't been listening.

Scottie tugged Libby's hand. "Let's go outdoors and play right now."

Grandma laughed. "Libby wants to dress and eat first, Scottie. You come with me for now. Libby won't be long."

Libby fingered her soft nightgown. "Where's Miss Miller?"

Grandma hesitated. "She went out about an hour ago. She said she had to see about . . . about your mother." Grandma touched Libby's cheek. "I'm sure that woman wasn't your mother. We know everyone in this town. Marie Dobbs does not live here."

"But she could be visiting!" cried Libby, wringing her hands. "She could've found out I was going to be here, then followed me to force me to live with her!"

"Why don't we just wait until Gwen gets back. You're getting nervous over nothing, honey. Get dressed and come eat. You'll feel better then."

Libby stood quietly as Grandma and Scottie walked out, closing the door softly. That woman was Mother! No one could look that much like Mother. Libby covered her pale face with trembling hands. Hot tears slipped down her cheeks. She had to talk to Miss Miller! Would she find Mother?

By the time Libby had forced down an egg and a piece of toast, Miss Miller walked in. Libby leaped up. What had Miss Miller learned? Libby's heart raced.

Miss Miller rested her hands on Libby's shoulders. "I asked around, but I couldn't find the woman we saw. No one has heard of Marie Dobbs. That woman probably looked like your mother and we assumed the worst. But, honey, I've agreed to stay here for my vacation. I'll be right here with you. If that was your mother, I'll take care of everything. Don't you worry about a thing. This is your vacation. I want you to enjoy it."

Tears glistened in Libby's eyes. "Thank you, Miss Miller. I'm glad you're going to stay."

Just then a tall man with light brown hair and hazel eyes walked in. Miss Miller gasped, her blue eyes wide. "Luke!" she whispered.

He held out his hands in surprise. "Gwen! How did you come to be here? I've been trying to get in touch with you."

"You have?" Miss Miller's face turned from white to bright red. Libby thought she was going to faint.

Libby listened in fascination. Miss Miller was stunned and could barely speak. The man Luke talked freely and looked at her like Dad looked just before he kissed Mom. Libby knew they had forgotten she was there.

"I had no idea you were related to these Johnsons or Libby's Johnsons," said Miss Miller faintly, her hand at her throat.

"Who's Libby?" asked Luke.

Libby wanted to sink through the floor. She hated for him to know she was only an aid kid living with the Johnsons. But Miss Miller explained it so nicely that Libby didn't blush as Luke held out his hand to her, welcoming her to the family.

"I guess I'm your Uncle Luke," he said with a grin that suddenly made him look a lot like Chuck. Only Luke was younger, taller, and leaner than Chuck. He had brown hair instead of red.

"I met Scottie," said Libby.

"Oh, yes, my son," he said with a laugh. "Scottie knows everyone or makes sure he meets everyone."

Libby saw the stricken look on Miss Miller's face.

"Is your wife with you?" asked Miss Miller in a tight voice.

Luke hesitated. "She died about two years ago."

"Oh. I'm sorry, Luke." She backed up against the table. "Two years! Oh, Luke!"

"I looked for you, Gwen." He ran his fingers through his hair. "Are you married yet?"

"No," she whispered.

Libby thought about what Miss Miller had said in the car. Was Luke the man she'd been in love with?

Scottie burst into the room. "Libby, are you done? I want to play outdoors." He stopped. "Hi, Pop. Libby's gonna take me outdoors."

Luke pulled his son against himself. "Scottie, I want you to meet a good friend of mine. Gwen Miller, Scottie Johnson." His voice was full of pride.

"I'm glad to meet you, Scottie," said Miss Miller.

"Will you come out and play, too?" asked Scottie with a grin. "I got a new truck and a new tractor. I'd let you play with them."

"Hold it, Scottie," said Luke, ruffling Scottie's

hair. "Gwen and I have a lot of talking to do. You take Libby and let me keep Gwen. You can't have all the girls, you know."

"Is she going to be my new mother?"

Miss Miller gasped.

"Go out and play," said Luke firmly.

"But you said we were going to look for my new mother," said Scottie.

"We'll talk about it later, son. Take Libby out in the yard. But put on your jacket. It's still chilly out."

Scottie looked at Miss Miller. "You tell Pop you want to be my new mother. I'm tired of waiting for him to find one."

"Scott Russell Johnson! Get out of here right now!" Luke smacked Scottie on the bottom. "Libby, will you take good care of him for me?"

"Yes. Is it OK if I take him to the park?" Libby edged toward the doorway to the hall. She knew Miss Miller was embarrassed.

"That's fine with me," said Luke. "Be home in time for lunch."

"We will," said Libby. Thankfully she took Scottie to the closet and took out their jackets. She couldn't wait to get away from Miss Miller and Luke. She felt funny listening to them and watching the way they looked at each other.

"Do you want the truck or tractor?" asked Scottie as he picked them up off the floor near the closet door.

Libby smiled. "Why don't we leave them here

for now. When we get back from the park we'll play with them." Suddenly she stopped. Yesterday on the way to the park she'd seen Mother. What if she saw her today without Miss Miller beside her? "Scottie, let's just play in the yard for now. We'll go to the park later."

Scottie's face fell. "I want to swing and go down the slide. Please, Libby."

She took a deep breath. Dad had said Jesus was always with her. Jesus would be with her in the park even if Mother was around. "All right, Scottie. We'll go to the park." Miss Miller had said that no one knew about Marie Dobbs. Maybe she'd been visiting for the day and was gone now. Besides, Libby realized suddenly, she could run fast. If Mother came to the park, she'd take Scottie's hand and quickly run back to the Johnsons'."

Libby looked down at Scottie's happy face as they walked into the bright sunlight. Scottie wanted a mother badly. She had one mother too many. Vera Johnson was the only mother she wanted.

A small dog behind a white picket fence barked at them. Scottie stopped to talk to it. Libby watched him with a smile. Suddenly she realized the little boy was her cousin—well, practically a cousin. Luke was her uncle. Uncle Luke. Cousin Scottie. She was gaining more relatives all the time.

"We're cousins, Scottie," said Libby happily.

Six
The chase

Scottie was as excited over the park as Libby knew he would be. He dashed from one thing to another, shouting and laughing happily. The park seemed tiny to Libby after the parks in the city. Nobody could get lost in this park. They had it all to themselves. A squirrel chattered from a tree branch near the green bench beside the water fountain. Did anyone ever feed him nuts?

"Help me slide," called Scottie as he ran around to climb up the tall slide.

Libby stood at the bottom with her hands out. She laughed at the look of scared delight on Scottie's face as he swooshed down the slide into her waiting arms.

"You take a turn, Libby," Scottie said excitedly. "I'll catch you."

Libby climbed up. She sat at the top, then swooshed down, almost knocking Scottie over. They laughed and laughed. Ben, Susan, Kevin, and Toby would have fun in this park.

Suddenly a big blue-gray cat zipped past Libby's legs. A small black dog raced after the cat, barking wildly. The dog's lead slithered through the grass like a long snake. Scottie jumped up and down, shouting for the dog to leave the cat alone.

An old lady sagged against the slide, puffing and panting. She pointed to the dog with a trembling hand. "Catch my dog. I can't run another step."

Libby dashed after the dog, with Scottie behind her. She lunged for the lead but just missed it. Quickly she leaped to her feet and raced around a few bushes. She lunged once again and caught the lead, pulling the dog up short, cutting off his wild barking. The cat streaked up a tree and sat on a limb, hissing. With his back arched and his fur fluffed out, he looked twice the size he really was.

Scottie dropped to the grass, laughing hard. "That was a fun chase." He shook his head at the dog. "Why did you do that, doggy? Don't chase that cat again."

Libby laughed as she walked the dog back to the tired woman who had found a bench to rest on. Libby was glad she'd been able to catch the dog. She handed the lead over to the tired woman.

The woman lifted the dog to her lap as she smiled tiredly at Libby. "Thank you, young lady. I don't know why you're not in school, but I'm glad you were here when I needed you." She hugged the dog. "Shame on you, Rochester. You know you aren't to chase cats. Just feel your little heart beating a mile a minute." She reached for her purse. "You youngsters helped me out today. I'd like to give you a little something."

Libby twisted her toe in the grass. Not long ago she would not have helped anyone in need. Now that she did, she didn't want to be paid for it. "We're glad we could help. We don't want any pay."

"Then I won't make you feel bad by trying to force you to take it." She pushed wisps of gray hair out of her wrinkled face. "Thank you again."

"You're welcome." Libby didn't know what to say further.

Scottie grabbed her hand and tugged. "Let's go swing."

With a mumbled goodbye, Libby ran across the park with Scottie. The sun felt hot on her head. She tugged off her jacket and flipped it over the end of the swings. She pushed Scottie back and forth until he squealed happily.

Loud yelling made Libby look across to the bench where the old woman sat with her dog. Another old woman stood beside the bench, shaking her fist at the woman sitting down.

"Where's Albert, Lena Perkins?" shouted the angry woman. Her long gray coat flapped around her black pants legs. "I saw your nasty little dog chasing my Albert. Where is he?"

44

Libby couldn't hear Mrs. Perkins answer, but she saw her pointing to them. The woman turned and glared right at Libby. Libby wanted to run away.

"Young lady," called Mrs. Perkins. "Would you help Mrs. LaDere find her cat?"

Mrs. LaDere hurried across the park, then stopped suddenly, staring at Libby as if she'd seen a ghost. Finally she said in a strangled voice, "Where is my Albert?"

Libby's mouth suddenly felt cotton dry. She didn't like the way Mrs. LaDere was staring at her. Was she grass-stained from catching the dog?

"Can't you talk? I want my cat!"

"He's . . . he's up that tree," said Libby hoarsely, pointing to the tree.

The woman stepped closer to Libby. "What's your name?"

"We can't talk to strangers," Scottie said loudly. "We can't take candy from a stranger and we can't talk to strangers. You're a stranger."

The woman's face darkened with anger. "You're too smart for your britches!" Abruptly she turned away and walked to the tree where Albert sat.

Scottie slipped his hand in Libby's as they watched Mrs. LaDere stop under the tree.

"Come, Albert," she called sweetly. "Come on, sweety. That mean dog won't chase you again." She held up her arms and coaxed and begged but Albert wouldn't budge. Finally Mrs.

45

LaDere sagged against the tree. Libby could see tears slide down the woman's wrinkled cheek. Her thin shoulders shook.

Libby felt sorry for the woman. She really should help get Albert down. But Mrs. LaDere made her feel very strange.

Dad had said often that to put God's Word into action was the proof of a true believer. Jesus would want her to help Mrs. LaDere. Still Libby hesitated. She closed her eyes and leaned against the cold steel of the swing set. Silently she asked Jesus to help her reach out to Mrs. LaDere.

Scottie rubbed his head against her arm. "Poor Albert can't get down," Scottie said sadly. "He might get hungry up there. Or he might go to sleep and fall from the tree."

Libby swallowed hard. "I'll help get Albert. Scottie, you stay here by the swings. I don't want Albert to jump on you if I scare him."

Scottie sank to the ground beside a leg of the swing set and Libby ran to Mrs. LaDere. Libby took a deep breath.

"I'll get Albert down for you," said Libby in a funny high voice that didn't sound like her own.

Mrs. LaDere looked up sharply. Hastily she dried her tears. "Albert hates strangers. Albert hates everyone but me."

"I'll get him down," said Libby. She grabbed a low branch and swung her leg over it, then scrambled up. Albert stared at her with his green cat eyes. Libby thought he was going to arch his back and hiss at her. Quietly she talked to him.

If she reached for him, would he scratch her? He was bigger than any cat she'd ever seen. Could she carry him down the tree?

"Don't hurt my Albert," called up Mrs. LaDere.

Slowly Libby reached for Albert. He allowed her to pick him up and hold him. He was almost as big as the dog that had chased him. "We're going down, Albert. Don't be scared. I won't drop you."

Carefully Libby climbed down, then dropped to the ground beside Mrs. LaDere.

"Albert. Albert," said Mrs. LaDere as she pulled him away from Libby and hugged him close. She kissed his face and shoulders. "We'll go home, Albert, and have a nice din-din."

Mrs. LaDere started across the park, then turned back. "You look like somebody I know," she said sharply. "Who are you?"

For some strange reason Libby didn't want to tell her. Finally the woman turned away and walked out of the park to a small white house. She disappeared inside with Albert still in her arms.

Libby jumped when Scottie slipped his hand in hers. "I brought your jacket," said Scottie. "I'm hungry. I want to go home."

Mrs. Perkins stopped in front of them, her dog's leash securely in her hand. "Don't mind Ruth LaDere. She's a cross old lady. Always has been. Always will be." She shook her head. "I think Albert's the only thing she loves. That's sad. I love my Rochester, but I love my family, too. Ruth LaDere doesn't love anyone."

Libby squirmed uncomfortably. She didn't know what to say.

"Come to think of it, you look a lot like her granddaughter. You don't happen to be any relation, do you?"

Libby shook her head. Maybe that's why Mrs. LaDere had looked at her so strangely.

"Thank you again for catching Rochester for me," said Mrs. Perkins. She tugged her coat around her. "I will keep a tight hold on him when I see Albert out in his yard." She walked slowly away with Rochester tugging at his leash.

A squirrel whisked from one tree to another. Scottie dashed after it, shouting to it. Libby laughed. Scottie couldn't run fast enough to catch a squirrel. She slipped on her jacket and followed Scottie. Finally he was tired of trying to find the squirrel. He stopped beside her, panting hard.

"I'm thirsty," he said, his thin chest heaving up and down.

"We'll get a drink in the fountain," said Libby, suddenly feeling very thirsty too.

Libby pressed the lever, then laughed as water squirted in Scottie's face. After he drank, she did. The water was cold and good.

A car, then a truck drove past, turning toward downtown. Libby watched them go. About a block away she saw a woman walking toward them. Libby's heart raced. The woman had bleached blonde hair and was dressed in tight blue pants and a sweater. It was Mother.

Libby grabbed Scottie's hand and tugged hard. "We got to get out of here, Scottie," she said wildly. "Run!"

"What's wrong, Libby?" he cried, his eyes wide.

But Libby didn't answer. She pulled him faster than his legs could go and he stumbled. She hauled him to his feet. She almost dropped his hand to run off without him. But she'd promised Uncle Luke she'd take good care of him.

"Hurry faster, Scottie," she cried in anguish. She could not allow Mother to see her. She had to get to the Johnsons' and tell Miss Miller that she'd seen Mother again. And she'd never go to the park again unless Miss Miller was with her! Oh, why had she left the Johnson farm? She'd beg Miss Miller to take her home. She couldn't stay in the same town with Mother! It wasn't safe.

Seven
Friend or enemy?

Miss Miller was walking around the yard when Libby reached home. Libby urged Scottie to go into the house.

"What is it, Libby?" asked Miss Miller as she caught Libby's trembling hand.

"I saw her again! We were in the park and I saw her!" Libby's chest heaved up and down. Her legs felt like rubber and she slumped to the grass.

Miss Miller knelt beside her and held her close. "She can't hurt you, Libby. Even if that woman is your mother, she can't hurt you. She can't take you. I'm here to take care of you. The Johnsons will protect you."

Libby clung tightly to Miss Miller. Her face pressed against Miss Miller's orange sweater. Finally she stopped trembling and pulled away. She sniffed back hot tears. "I want to go home. I want to go home right now, today. Will you take me? I will be safe on the Johnson farm. Oh, please, take me home!"

"Libby. Libby, listen to me." Miss Miller took Libby's face in her hands. She studied Libby's scared hazel eyes and trembling pointed chin. "Running away won't help. It never does. This woman you saw, we saw, might not be your mother. A lot of women bleach their hair and are tall and slender. And a lot of women dress like your mother always does with tight clothes and a lot of makeup. I want to find this woman so we know for sure."

Libby groaned.

"If this woman isn't your mother, then you can enjoy the rest of your visit." Miss Miller stood up and lifted Libby with her. "Let's sit on the porch steps and talk."

Libby sniffed hard as they walked to the porch. She felt dizzy and sick. Why couldn't Miss Miller understand?

After several minutes of talking Miss Miller was able to convince Libby to stay at least long enough to discover the real identity of the woman.

Miss Miller brushed an ant off her pant leg. "I want you to be very brave, Libby. I think if I sit in the park I'll be able to find her. We saw her near there yesterday, and you did again today. She could be visiting someone. Then again if it is someone who looks like your mother, I will learn her name and where she lives."

"But if she sees you she might hide. She might be after me!" Libby locked her fingers together so tightly her knuckles ached.

"We'll handle it, Libby." Miss Miller smiled and patted Libby's hands. "Everything will work out just fine. Wait and see."

Libby looked up to see Uncle Luke walking down the sidewalk toward them. She felt Miss Miller grow tense.

Miss Miller jumped up. "I'm going around back for a while, then to the park."

Libby waited for Luke. Why had Miss Miller suddenly hurried away? Was she scared of Uncle Luke?

"Hi, Libby," said Luke, sitting beside her, his long legs straight out. "Where's Scottie?"

"In with Grandma."

"Did you have fun in the park?"

Libby told him about the time in the park. She didn't tell him about Mrs. LaDere's strange remark that Libby looked like someone she knew. And she didn't tell him about seeing Mother. She just couldn't.

Luke rested his hands on his knees and leaned forward. "Where did Gwen go?"

"For a walk." Why did his voice sound funny when he asked about Miss Miller?

He stood up and slipped his hands in his pockets. "I think I'll find her. I've got to straighten something out."

Libby watched him walk around the house. A robin sang on a tree branch. Libby heard Scottie shouting from inside the house. She stood up. Maybe Scottie wanted to play with his truck and tractor.

Just as she stepped inside, Scottie ran down the steps. He held out his hand to show Libby a tiny grand piano.

"Look, Libby. See the tiny piano!"

"Scottie!" Libby grabbed the piano. "Don't you touch that piano. It's mine!"

Big tears filled Scottie's eyes and splashed down to his hands.

Libby held the piano tightly as she glared at Scottie. "You might have broken it! It's not a toy, Scottie."

A sob escaped him and his shoulders stiffened as he tried to keep from crying aloud. He looked very small standing in front of Libby. His jeans were grass-stained. His blue shirt had juice stain down the front of it. He stared down at his dusty tennis shoes.

Libby's anger vanished. She bent down to him. "I'm sorry, Scottie. I shouldn't have yelled at you. Let me show you the piano." She tried to get him to talk to her but he turned away. Finally Libby gave up. Slowly she walked to her room, the piano in her hand. When would she learn to control her temper? Scottie hadn't hurt the piano. He didn't know it was important to her. He probably didn't know it was hers.

She placed the piano on the dresser next to her brush. She sighed unhappily. She remembered all the times Mother had yelled at her, had beat her for doing something she thought was wrong. Was she going to be just like Mother? Libby shivered as she remembered the

53

time Mother had whipped her with an extension cord.

"I won't be like Mother!" she whispered, her hands pressed to her heart. She remembered Dad telling her that when she'd accepted Jesus as Savior she'd become a new person. The old person was dead. The new person Jesus had made her into couldn't be like Mother. Libby sank to her bed with a relieved sigh. "Thank you, Jesus," she whispered. "Thank you for my new life. Forgive me for getting mad at Scottie and yelling at him. I'm sorry. Help me not to do it again. And Jesus, don't let Mother find me and take me away from the Johnson family."

Libby looked up as Scottie walked slowly into the room. "Want to play with me?" he asked quietly.

"Sure," she said, smiling and holding out her hand to him.

"I'm sorry for touching your piano. I won't do it again." He stood with his hands at his sides, his feet apart. Something about him reminded her of Kevin.

Libby hugged him close. "You can look at my piano anytime you want." She told him about Joe giving her the piano and why it meant so much to her. Scottie listened intently. He seemed to enjoy listening to Libby. She told him about Toby and Dusty, then about Snowball, the filly the family had given her on her twelfth birthday.

"Pop said we are going to visit Uncle Chuck

and his family soon. Can I ride Dusty?"

"Sure you can," answered Libby. She brushed his red-gold hair back. It felt like soft baby hair. "Shall we go outdoors and play with your truck and tractor now? We'll pretend we're on the farm with them."

Scottie dashed to the door with a shout. Libby followed with a pleased smile. She and Scottie were friends again.

The sun felt very warm on Libby as she sat in the yard with Scottie. Several children ran past. A few of them stared at Libby and Scottie. One girl stopped on the sidewalk. Libby looked at her and gasped in surprise. The girl slowly walked across the grass, her eyes wide.

"You look like me," said the girl in a strange voice.

"You look like *me!*" exclaimed Libby, jumping to her feet. The girl standing in front of her was a little older and not as thin. She had the same brown hair, pointed chin, and narrow face. Only the girl had blue eyes instead of hazel.

"Are we related?" She rested her hands on her hips and tilted her head. "My name is Tammy LaDere."

Scottie jumped to his feet. "I'm Scottie and this is Libby. My pop is Luke Johnson and hers is Chuck Johnson."

The girl shook her head. "We might never know if we're related. Are you living here now? I haven't seen you before."

"I'm visiting Grandma and Grandpa Johnson

for two weeks." Libby didn't know what to think of Tammy. She talked fast and breathlessly.

"I'm thirteen."

"I'm twelve."

"Do you have any boyfriends?"

Libby flushed. Was Joe Wilkens her boyfriend? Finally she shrugged.

"I have two, but I'm going with Ted Stevens. He's fifteen." Tammy trailed her finger through the birdbath as she smiled dreamily. "We're going to a drive-in tonight with Ted's brother and his girl friend." She looked up sharply at Libby. "Have you ever been to an R rated movie?" She didn't wait for an answer. "I think it would be fun to be friends with a girl who looks so much like me. Would you like to be friends? Do you always have to have this little boy around you? Can you ever go off by yourself?"

Libby didn't know if she liked Tammy or not. But it might be fun to have a friend who looked so much like her.

"You don't talk much, do you? Well, I talk enough for ten people, my grandma always says. I'm staying with my grandma a while. So is Mom." Tammy leaned close to Libby. "Mom wasn't married when she had me. Mom was never married. I always tell that right off so it doesn't get in the way of friendship. That's why I don't think we'll ever know if we're related. I don't know my father."

"Maybe we could walk downtown together sometime," said Libby.

"I could fix you up with a boyfriend if you want, Libby. Or would you get into too much trouble with your family?"

"I don't want a boyfriend," said Libby, trying hard not to blush. This girl would get along just fine with Brenda Wilkens. Both of them talked about boys a lot.

"Play with me, Libby," said Scottie, tugging at her hand.

Libby hesitated. She enjoyed playing with Scottie, but it did get a little boring. "I'll play with you later, Scottie." She looked at Tammy. "We could go ask Grandma for some cookies and milk."

"Sounds good. I'm hungry. And if I go home, Grandma will complain and yell at me for teasing her cat." Tammy sighed as they walked inside. "You wouldn't believe what I have to put up with at home. Sometimes I wonder why I stay."

Libby introduced Tammy to Grandma, then sat at the kitchen table and ate chocolate cookies and drank cold milk. Grandma was surprised that they looked alike.

"Your grandma is nicer than mine," said Tammy as Grandma walked out of the kitchen. "But she probably makes you mad sometimes, doesn't she?"

Libby couldn't imagine being mad at Grandma.

"Tomorrow after school I'll stop here and we'll walk downtown together. We might meet some boys to take us for a ride."

"I don't want to do that. You can go by yourself."

Tammy laughed. "Just wait until you're thirteen. You'll change your mind. But if you don't want to ride around with boys, then we won't."

"I think I should go play with Scottie now. Want to play?"

Tammy sniffed in disdain. "I'm not a child, Libby." She walked to the door. "See you tomorrow."

Libby watched her leave and wondered if she really wanted to be friends. Tammy acted like girls she'd seen when she lived with Mother. Those girls had always been in trouble. Would Tammy get into trouble?

Libby sighed. Would Tammy turn out to be a friend or an enemy?

Eight
Who is
Phyllis LaDere?

Libby looked at the row of jewelry that Tammy was studying intently. Libby liked the gold chains and the necklace with hearts hooked together. It was similar to the one she was wearing. Her real dad had sent it to her in a secret puzzle box. Could she tell Tammy about that? Tammy had shared several secrets with her.

Tammy held up a fine gold chain. "This is the one I want." She looked at the price tag and replaced it with a sigh. "I don't have enough money." She smiled. "But I'll tell Mom about it and she'll get it for me. I can always manage to get what I want from her. I think it's because she knows if she keeps me happy I'll stay out of her way."

The girls walked out of the store and down the quiet street. Only three other people were on the street. It seemed strange to Libby. She had never been in a small town before. Stores lined only two blocks, then the residential district started.

Trees shaded the quiet streets. Lawns were well kept and green. Many of the homes had flowers growing in the front yards near the sidewalk.

When they were about a block from the park, Tammy nudged Libby. "See that woman walking out of that green house? That's Mom."

Libby's heart raced and her legs grew almost too weak to hold her. It was Mother that Tammy pointed to! But how could Tammy's mother be Mother? Libby's head spun and she shivered violently.

"What's wrong?" asked Tammy, grabbing her arm. "Are you going to faint?"

Libby licked her dry lips. She wanted to turn and run as Mother walked toward her. She seemed glued to the spot. Was she having a nightmare? Would she wake up to find she was home safe in her own bed?

"Hi, Mom," said Tammy brightly. "Libby, this is my mother, Phyllis LaDere."

Libby stared. She wasn't Mother! She looked a lot like Mother, but she wasn't! Libby felt weak with relief. Then she noticed the intent look from Phyllis LaDere and she backed away in fright.

Suddenly Phyllis LaDere grabbed Libby and jerked her close. "You're coming with me."

"Do you know Libby, Mom?" asked Tammy with a frown.

"I know her."

Libby gasped at the anger in the woman's voice. Her sharp nails dug into Libby's bare arm. What did she want? Where was she taking her?

Tammy almost ran to keep up with her mother's fast pace as she dragged Libby along. "Mom, did you notice how much we look alike, Libby and me?"

"I noticed."

With a quick twist and a downward jerk Libby broke free. She sped away, her heart racing so fast she thought it would leap out of her rib cage. Shivers ran up and down her spine as she heard the *slap slap* of running feet behind her. She ran into the park, trying to cut across to turn back toward the Johnsons. Where was Miss Miller? She said she'd sit in the park to try to find Mother.

Suddenly Libby tripped and sprawled in the grass. She struggled to get up, but Tammy leaped on her, pinning her to the ground.

"I got her, Mom," shouted Tammy, almost breaking Libby's eardrum. "I won't let her get away."

"You're stupid for running away from me," said Phyllis LaDere angrily. She jerked Libby to her feet. "You're going home with me. I want to know all about you."

Roughly she pulled Libby across the street right into the little white house where the woman lived who owned Albert the cat. Libby shivered as she remembered how Mrs. LaDere had looked at her. This whole family was crazy. What did they want with her?

"Mother!" called Phyllis LaDere as she slammed the door behind them. "I have someone I want you to meet."

Mrs. LaDere walked toward them, Albert snuggled in her arms. She nodded with a grumble. "I saw her the other day. I wondered about her."

Phyllis pushed Libby into a chair, then stood over her with an angry scowl. "Now, who are you and why are you in town?"

"Her name's Libby Johnson," said Tammy, sitting on the edge of the couch. "She's staying with her grandparents."

Phyllis spun around and glared at Tammy. "Shut up! Who asked you, Miss Smarty Britches?"

Libby leaped from the chair, but before she could get away, Phyllis grabbed her and shoved her back down. "You're not going anywhere until you tell me about your family. Is your mother Marie Dobbs?"

Libby gasped as she cringed lower in the chair. "Tell me!"

Libby swallowed hard and nodded.

"I knew it!" Phyllis turned to her mother. "Didn't you?"

The old woman sat on the couch with Albert on her lap. "I kinda figured so. Nobody could look that much like our family without being part of it."

Libby groaned. She belonged to this family. That was the worst thing in the world to have happen to her!

Phyllis leaned close to Libby. "Where is your mother? Is she in town with you?"

Libby licked her dry lips. "She's . . . she's in Australia."

"No wonder I couldn't find her! I might have known! Well, I'll get her yet!"

"Don't get started on that, Phyllis," said Mrs. LaDere tiredly.

Phyllis paced the room. The minute she was near the window Libby leaped to her feet and raced for the door. She had to get away! She grabbed the doorknob but Phyllis was on her, jerking her away.

"Get back in that chair. I'm not finished with you yet." Roughly she pushed Libby across the room and back into the chair.

"Don't get so rough, Mom," said Tammy, nervously twisting her fingers. "What do you want with Libby? What has she done to you?"

"Shut up, Tammy," snapped Phyllis. "If you can't keep your mouth quiet for a while, then go to your room." Phyllis tugged her gold sweater over her dark blue pants. She fingered a heavy chain around her neck.

Libby opened her eyes wide to keep the tears from falling. She would not cry in front of these people, these strangers who seemed to think they were family. The Johnsons didn't even know there were people like this.

"Is she my cousin?" asked Tammy in surprise as she stared at Libby.

Mrs. LaDere nodded grimly. "I wouldn't be too happy about it if I were you. She's probably just like her mother. Or that no-good runaway father."

Libby's head seemed to spin. A bitter taste filled her mouth. With a shudder she looked at the old woman who was her real grandmother. Why couldn't she be like Grandma Feuder? This woman was hard and cold and never smiled unless she was looking at or touching her Albert.

Phyllis pushed her hair back from her face with short, jerky motions. "Marie took my man and my money when she left here. And she's going to pay for it!" She grabbed Libby's arm, her fingernails biting into soft flesh. "When is Marie coming back from Australia?"

"I don't know," whispered Libby in terror.

Phyllis released Libby's arm and leaned down close to her. Her breath smelled like stale tobacco. "I can't get my man back, but I'll get my money back even if I have to get it from you."

Libby cringed against the soft back of the chair, her eyes wide with fear. "I . . . I don't have any money."

"What about the family you live with? They might have."

They did have money, but it would be terrible if they had to pay Mother's debts!

Phyllis spun around to Tammy. "You saw the family. Do they have money?"

Tammy stood behind the couch, her face white. "I don't know. But Libby doesn't live with them. She's only here on a vacation. She lives with another Johnson family on a farm." Tammy looked thoughtful. "But her Uncle Luke might have money. He drives a big car and dresses rich."

Phyllis gasped. "Luke! Luke Johnson is your uncle?"

Libby nodded reluctantly. What did Phyllis want with Uncle Luke? Would she find a way to take money from him?

Phyllis fingered the chain around her neck. Her eyes were narrowed thoughtfully. "I heard his wife died, but I didn't think he'd come back to this hick town after being away so long. We once were very good friends."

"Only until he saw that you wouldn't go along with that religion of his," snapped Mrs. LaDere. "And he sure won't take up with the likes of you now."

"Oh, I wouldn't say that. He might like me with blonde hair."

Libby closed her eyes. Blood pounded in her ears. She opened her eyes and looked around her. It had to be a nightmare.

Suddenly Albert jumped off Mrs. LaDere's lap

and walked over to Libby. He rubbed against her leg and she rested her hand on his big blue-gray head. She felt better just being able to touch him. Albert jumped up and curled up in her lap, purring loudly.

Mrs. LaDere gasped, eyeing Libby strangely. "Albert don't like anybody but me. He never did that before. How did you get him to do that?"

"What does it matter?" snapped Phyllis impatiently. "You and your cat, Mother! I'll be glad when he's dead!"

"Don't say that!" cried Libby, protectively covering Albert with her hands.

Mrs. LaDere stood up, her thin body trembling with rage. "Phyllis, I've had all I'm going to take from you. Get out. And let that girl go back where she belongs." She pointed shakily at Libby.

Angrily Phyllis shoved Albert off Libby's lap and jerked her to her feet. "I'm taking you home right now, my girl. This will give me a perfect reason for seeing Luke again."

Libby stumbled outdoors with Phyllis LaDere beside her. The bright sun made her blink. A dog barked in the park. Phyllis kept a tight hold on Libby's arm.

"You are going to walk along with me as if we are friends," she snapped. "And you will not tell your family how I treated you. Understand?"

Libby defiantly lifted her pointed chin. Her hazel eyes flashed. "I will tell them everything. And they'll see that you never touch me again!"

Phyllis stopped and turned Libby to her. Her blue eyes were dark with rage. "If you tell them I'll . . . I'll. . . ." She frowned thoughtfully, then chuckled dryly. "You think a lot about that cat of Mother's. If you say one word to Luke or the others, I'll see that Albert doesn't live."

"You wouldn't! You couldn't!" But Libby could see that she meant every word. Libby's shoulders sagged. Tears pricked her eyes.

"I'll kill Albert if you don't do exactly as I say."

Slowly Libby walked beside Phyllis LaDere across the park and down the sidewalk.

Nine
Family

Uncle Luke and Miss Miller sat side by side in lawn chairs, their heads close together, as Libby and Phyllis LaDere walked into the yard.

Libby wanted to run to Miss Miller and beg for protection, but she didn't dare. She took a deep breath and forced her hands to stop trembling. Miss Miller must not guess that anything was wrong.

"Hello, Luke," Phyllis said softly, a smile on her red lips.

Luke jumped lightly to his feet. "Phyllis! It's been a long time." He turned and helped Miss Miller up. "Phyllis LaDere, Gwen Miller."

Miss Miller gasped, then covered it with a cough. She looked quickly at Libby.

Before Libby could speak, Phyllis said, "Can you believe that this little girl is niece to both of us? She's mine by birth and yours by custody."

"Is that right?" Uncle Luke scratched his

68

head. "What a small world. No wonder she thought you looked like her mother."

"Marie and I are sisters." Phyllis laughed as she looked at Miss Miller. "And how do you fit into the picture?"

Libby watched Miss Miller hesitate. "I'm a family friend." She turned to Libby. "Would you please tell your grandma that you're home? She was getting a little worried about you."

Phyllis touched Libby's arm and smiled sweetly. "Don't forget that we want to see a lot of you while you're visiting." She beamed at Luke and Miss Miller. "Now that we found Libby, we want to share her with you. You don't mind, do you? Libby has another family right here in town. Me, Tammy, and her grandmother. Not to mention Albert."

Libby's heart almost stopped, then raced frantically. She knew what the woman was saying.

Phyllis tapped Libby's nose. "I know how much you love your grandma's cat." She looked up at Luke and Miss Miller. "Did you know that Libby loves animals? She already made friends with Albert, my mother's big cat."

Libby turned and ran to the house, her ears ringing and a cold sick feeling in her stomach. She leaned against the hall door, her chest heaving. What could she do? How could she stop Phyllis LaDere?

"Oh, Libby!" Grandma stopped in the hall. "I'm so glad you're back. Why, what's wrong with you? You're pale and shivering. Did you catch a chill?" She touched Libby's forehead and cheeks. Her hand smelled like hand lotion.

Libby looked at Grandma. She looked like a grandma should, short and plump and full of love. Libby flung her arms around her, pressing her face against Grandma's neck. "I love you, Grandma."

"I love you, too, Libby." Grandma sounded puzzled, but she held Libby tightly until Libby pulled away.

"Where are Scottie and Grandpa?" She forced her voice to sound as normal as possible.

"They went fishing. Grandpa wanted to take you, but you didn't get home in time. I hope you aren't too disappointed." Grandma brushed Libby's hair back from her face. "Are you sure you're all right? You look a little pale."

"I'm just fine, Grandma. I guess I need some lunch." She didn't know if she could eat, but she wanted Grandma to stop looking at her so closely.

"You go wash and I'll fix you a sandwich. Will grilled cheese be all right?"

Libby nodded, then stood there as Grandma hurried to the kitchen. She turned as the front door closed. Miss Miller stood there, her head down, her cheeks flushed. She looked up and saw Libby.

"Oh, Libby! That woman is your aunt! Were you frightened when you saw her?" Miss Miller clasped her hands and shivered.

"At first I wanted to run away," said Libby slowly. She had to be very careful with Miss Miller. "Tammy was with me and said she was her mother. At a close look you can see the difference. But they do look a lot alike."

"And act alike!"

Libby nodded.

"Luke seems to enjoy talking to her," Miss Miller said stiffly. She walked across the hall, then back. "He's acting as if they're dear old friends! Not once has he considered your feelings." Then she whispered, "Nor mine."

"I . . . I have to go wash for lunch," said Libby, backing away.

"Wait! Can you truthfully tell me you want to visit back and forth with that family as she said? Do you really want to spend a couple of nights with Tammy?"

Libby searched frantically for an answer. "Well, they are family."

"I refuse to allow you to see them!" Miss Miller's blue eyes snapped with anger. "I know what it will do to you."

Libby lifted her chin defiantly. "You can't stop me! You're not my boss." Libby hated to see the hurt look on Miss Miller's face.

"I can ask the Johnsons to refuse to allow you to see them!"

Libby stuffed her trembling hands into her pockets. "You're just jealous. You're afraid Phyllis will take Uncle Luke away from you. And you want him for yourself!" Libby wanted to stuff

71

the words back in her mouth. Tears stung her own eyes as she saw Miss Miller's eyes fill with tears. But she couldn't risk doing anything to anger Phyllis LaDere. Libby turned and walked upstairs, her back stiff. Tears slipped down her cheeks. She wouldn't stop or turn when Miss Miller called to her. She didn't dare let Miss Miller see her cry.

Weakly Libby leaned against her closed bedroom door. She must think of a plan to stop Phyllis LaDere from hurting her new family. And from killing Albert! Her mind was blank. Ben or Kevin could have thought up a perfect plan. If only they were here! But that wouldn't work. She wouldn't be able to tell them either.

"Libby, lunch is ready," Grandma called up the steps.

Libby took a deep breath as she opened her door. "Be right down." Quickly she splashed cold water on her face and washed her hands. The girl in the mirror looked back at her very solemnly. "Can't you ever stay out of trouble?" whispered Libby. She made a face, then walked out.

The red fruit punch helped wash down the sandwich. Libby tried to visit normally with Grandma, but it was impossible.

"I think it would be good if you went to bed early tonight, Libby." Grandma once again felt her forehead and cheeks. "You just don't look or act right. Are you homesick, honey?"

Libby forced a smile. "I'm all right,

Grandma." Libby wanted to be able to share how she really felt, but she didn't dare.

"Libby, I don't know how to say this." Grandma stopped. Nervously she pleated her apron. "I don't think I like you associating with people like the LaDeres. I know they're your real family, but you were put in a foster home because of the way your mother treated you. I would think seeing the LaDeres would bring back a lot of old hurts."

Libby clenched her hands tightly in her lap. "I can't let old hurts stop me, Grandma."

"That's very mature of you, honey. Just don't get in so deep with these people that you get new hurts." Grandma pushed her fingers through her wavy gray hair. Her round cheeks looked flushed and warm. "Libby, if you ever need to talk, I'm here to listen."

Libby swallowed hard. "Thanks, Grandma." She wanted to snuggle close to Grandma and tell her everything. What would happen if she did? Would Grandma know of a way to keep Phyllis from killing Albert?

Libby jumped up, thanking Grandma for lunch. She could not stay in here. If she wasn't careful she'd be telling everything. Quickly she set her lunch dishes in the sink. "I'm going outdoors."

"Just don't overdo it. Vera wouldn't forgive me if you got sick."

Libby rushed out the kitchen door into the

backyard. She took great gulps of fresh air. She would not cry!

Slowly she walked around the house. She peeked around the corner, then sighed in relief. Phyllis LaDere was gone. Only Luke and Miss Miller were there, standing near each other talking.

"That woman is a phony," snapped Miss Miller, her hands on her hips. She looked very pretty dressed in blue jeans and a light blue sweater.

"Gwen. Gwen. You can't judge her by her sister's actions." Luke tried to slide his arm around her waist, but she knocked it away.

"I most certainly can! She was putting on a big, sweet act for your benefit! And you fell for it." She sighed impatiently. "I'll admit she is slightly pretty, but I don't expect you to be taken in by a pretty face and a good body."

Luke laughed, but it sounded strained to Libby. She knew she should leave and not listen to a private conversation, but she just had to hear what Miss Miller said.

"Luke Johnson, couldn't you see the look on Libby's face while that woman talked to her? Something is very wrong. And I mean to find out what it is!" She shook her brown hair out of her face. "If you refuse to help, then I'll do it on my own."

"And how do you expect to do it? Play spy games?" Luke sounded very impatient and angry. "I feel sorry for the woman. I always did. She had a baby when she was no more than fourteen years old. Do you know how hard that was for her? She could've given the baby up for adoption, but she didn't. She chose to keep her and raise her." Luke shoved his hands into his pockets. "Her mother was always mean to her. Now Phyllis is taking care of her. I admire that. Phyllis has the responsibility of an old woman and a young girl. She needs a friend. And I intend to be one."

Miss Miller's eyes snapped. "I'm sure you do! But that woman wants more than a friend, Luke."

"You're jealous, Gwen," he snapped.

Libby wanted to yell for them to stop fighting.

"Why should I be jealous? You're nothing to me, Luke Johnson. You walked away from me about five years ago to marry another woman. I have forgotten about you completely!" Her face was pale and her eyes large and haunted. "My concern right now is for Libby. I will not allow her to be hurt."

"I won't either. Not even by you."

"What's that supposed to mean?"

Libby leaned weakly against the side of the house. She thought she was going to throw up.

Luke stepped back from Miss Miller. "I won't let you keep that girl from her real family just because you have a crazy wild idea."

"And just how will you stop me?"

He laughed dryly. "Gwen, I could stop you so easily if I put my mind to it."

Libby turned and crept away. She couldn't

stand to hear another word. Why couldn't her life ever run smoothly? Why did she always ruin everything for everyone? She sank down on the back step and covered her face with her icy hands.

Ten
Family picnic

Reluctantly Libby walked downstairs. She
didn't want to face anyone today. Miss Miller
had acted very stiff and formal all last night.
Libby had wanted to say something to make her
feel better. Libby sighed unhappily. This
vacation was not turning out good at all. She
tugged her green sweatshirt down over her jeans.

"Good morning, Libby." Grandma smiled
cheerfully, her round face beaming happily. She
was dressed in black pants and jacket. "We have
a wonderful day planned today. Gwen and I
looked outdoors and saw how warm and beautiful
it is. So, Libby, we're going on a picnic to the
state park."

Libby looked quickly at Miss Miller. She was
actually smiling as if no bad words had passed
between them. Libby was so relieved that she
smiled too.

"Libby! Libby!" cried Scottie, rushing into the room. His hair was tousled and his cheeks red. "We're going on a picnic today. But we can't go swimming. Pop says it's too cold for swimming. But I don't have to wear my jacket. It's too warm for that." He tugged Libby's hand. "Hurry up and eat so we can leave."

Libby allowed him to pull her to the kitchen. She fixed herself a bowl of cornflakes and a piece of toast. Grandma poured her a glass of orange juice.

Grandpa walked in and tapped her on the head. "We're going on a picnic today, Elizabeth. Luke and I have the car packed and ready."

Libby laughed. "It won't take me long to eat."

Grandpa kissed her cheek. "It had better not. I want to get in a little fishing, too. I put in a pole for you."

Libby didn't know if she could stand to catch a fish on a sharp hook. Would it hurt his mouth? But she told Grandpa she'd try fishing.

"Gwen and I are going hiking," said Grandma, sliding her arm around Grandpa's waist. "And if Libby doesn't want to fish with you, she can hike with us."

"I'd like that," said Libby. By this time she was so excited that she could hardly eat. Scottie kept after her until finally she rinsed out her bowl and glass. She dabbed her mouth with a napkin and told him she was ready to leave.

"I'm gonna catch ten fish today and eat them

all," said Scottie as he scampered to the waiting car.

Luke stood beside the driver's side talking to Miss Miller. Libby could tell by her face that she wasn't happy with Uncle Luke. He turned and greeted Libby with a wide grin and cheerful good morning.

"I have a wonderful surprise for you, Libby," he said, his eyes twinkling.

"I know," said Libby, laughing. "We're going on a picnic."

"That's not all. Your aunt and cousin are going to meet us at the park. We're going to have a double family picnic for you." He smiled as if he was doing Libby a favor.

Libby felt as if she'd been kicked in the stomach. She tried her best to keep smiling. She looked at Miss Miller, then quickly away. Miss Miller knew how she really felt! What should she do? Miss Miller must not know!

"Load up, everyone," called Luke cheerfully. "We have a wonderful day ahead of us." He opened the door for Miss Miller to slide in front with him, but she climbed into the back. He frowned, but kept quiet. Grandma and Grandpa sat in front with Luke. Libby, Miss Miller, and Scottie sat in the back.

Libby peeked out the corner of her eye at Miss Miller. She looked so unhappy! Libby tried to think of something to say. She couldn't. Scottie chattered most of the way until Luke scolded him for talking so much. He sat back and looked at picture books, not minding that he had to stop talking. Several times Luke asked Miss Miller something. Each time she answered in a brisk, businesslike voice. Finally Luke quit trying. He pushed an eight-track tape in and music filled the car.

Libby leaned back and closed her eyes while the music drifted around her. She smelled Miss Miller's nice perfume. Scottie squirmed restlessly beside her.

Finally Luke pulled into the park. Tall pine trees surrounded tables, benches, and a large play area.

Scottie jumped out of the car and ran to a nearby table. "We'll eat here. I want a cookie. Can I have a cookie, Grandma?"

Libby helped carry the things to the table while Grandma hunted for the cookies. Nervously Libby looked around for Phyllis and Tammy. Were they here? What did their car look like?

Children ran, shouting and laughing, in the play area. Smoke billowed from cook pots. A woman walked past pushing a baby in a blue and yellow stroller.

"Libby! Libby, I saw a snake," cried Scottie, dashing across the grass.

Libby shivered. She didn't like snakes. "Don't let it bite you, Scottie," she said as she rushed toward him.

He laughed. "It won't bite me. Pop says I'm too tough."

Miss Miller walked up to Libby. "Scottie, run over to talk to Grandma while I talk to Libby, please."

Libby didn't want him to leave her alone with Miss Miller.

"Libby, I know you quite well after all this time." Miss Miller slid her hand in Libby's arm and slowly walked her away from the picnic table. "I know that something is wrong between you and Phyllis LaDere. I also know you are too frightened to talk about it."

Libby gulped. She could barely breathe.

"Last night I asked the Lord to help me solve your problem. And Libby, he *will* help me. I think that you've been so involved that you've forgotten that you're not alone in anything. You have us and you have your heavenly Father." Miss Miller rubbed Libby's arm. "I know that you can't say anything to me. But remember to put your problems in God's care. He knows who you are and where you are at all times. He will help you even when you think your situation is impossible."

Libby's heart leaped. Would God help find a way to keep Phyllis from killing Albert? Why hadn't she thought to pray about it? And right there as they walked along, Libby silently asked her heavenly Father to take care of Albert and the mess she was in. She smiled. She didn't know how he would take care of it, but she knew he would.

"When Phyllis and Tammy come, just remember that I'll have an eye on you. I won't let on to Phyllis that I know anything is up. But, Libby, I know something is wrong. Luke can't see it, but I can. No matter how loud you say that everything is fine, I won't believe you. I'm here to help you, Libby. And I mean to do just that no matter what Luke Johnson says."

Libby hugged Miss Miller wordlessly.

"They just drove in, Libby." Miss Miller fingered the chain around her neck. "We'll go greet them as if nothing is wrong. Smile, Libby. We do not want that woman to know she worries us."

Libby smiled. She greeted Tammy politely. Didn't they know how to dress for a picnic? Phyllis wore a soft, silky pink dress and Tammy wore white pants and a white and yellow top.

"Want to go for a hike?" asked Tammy as she slid her wire bracelets up and down her arm.

Libby looked questioningly at Grandma. She nodded yes. Libby knew she had done it reluctantly.

"Wait until after we eat," said Luke from the grill. "This is almost ready for hamburgers and hot dogs."

Phyllis walked over to him holding out a bag. "I brought chicken, too. Nothing tastes better than barbecued chicken over a grill."

Libby walked away so she wouldn't have to

listen to Phyllis and Luke. She saw Miss Miller sit at the table with Grandma.

"Let's go find some boys to talk to," said Tammy excitedly. "We'll see if we can find two who will walk with us after we eat." She turned to Libby. "Have you ever been kissed?"

Libby frowned. "That's a dumb thing to talk about." She walked around a water fountain. "Why didn't your grandma come with you?"

"Your grandma, too, don't forget." Tammy shook her head. Her curls bounced. "Isn't it funny to think we have the same grandma?" Tammy pulled a pine needle off a tree. "She's at home with Albert. She still can't believe that her cat would go to anyone else. She thinks you must have had a smell of catnip on you or something."

Libby could've told her about the animals at home that she took care of because they liked to be around her, but she didn't think Tammy would be interested.

"My mom wants to marry Luke Johnson," said Tammy with a sigh. "I sure don't want that little boy Scottie for a brother. I'd be stuck baby-sitting all the time."

Libby couldn't think of anything worse than Phyllis marrying Uncle Luke.

"Luke's different from the men Mom goes with. I've tried to figure out what makes him different, but I can't." She frowned. "Grandma says it's his religion. Do you know about his religion, Libby?"

"I know he believes the Bible and lives by it," said Libby.

"Would he marry someone like my mother?"

Libby frowned. If she answered yes, she'd be in trouble and if she answered no, she would be in worse trouble if Tammy repeated it. "Why don't you ask Uncle Luke?"

"I might do that." Tammy sat on a swing and slowly pushed herself.

Libby sat beside her. The gentle motion made her feel better. She wanted Tammy to talk about something else. Would Tammy like to hear about Snowball and Star and Apache Girl? Did she like horses?

"Oh, look! There's a cute boy over there." She jumped up. "I'm going over to talk to him." She walked away, her head held high. She stopped beside the boy. Libby couldn't hear what she said, but she could tell Tammy wasn't a bit shy or nervous. The boy seemed to like talking to Tammy.

Libby pushed her swing higher and higher until the wind whipped her hair. She went so high she could see over the top of the bar. She stopped pumping and slowly coasted to a gentle motion.

"Why didn't you come with me to talk to that boy?" asked Tammy as she leaned against the leg of the swing set. "His name is Bob and he's fifteen. He liked me. I could tell. He wants to take me for a walk later."

"I don't want to go!" said Libby sharply.

Tammy stamped her foot. "We sure won't have any fun if all you think about is being good. Let's go see if it's time to eat. I'm hungry."

Libby sighed in relief as they walked back to the picnic table where Grandpa sat with a cup of coffee.

Eleven
Caught!

Libby studied the checkerboard, then finally made her move. She grinned at Uncle Luke as he frowned. He had his hands on his knees as he leaned over the board.

"You know that you ruined my plan, don't you, young lady?" Uncle Luke shook his head and pretended to be very angry. "I don't play checkers unless I win."

"Neither do I," said Libby, laughing. The afternoon sunlight streamed through the window across the checkerboard. "And this time I'll win. You beat Miss Miller twice, and so it's your turn to lose." Libby smiled across the room where Miss Miller sat reading a book. Her nose was a little sunburned from yesterday's picnic.

"He's just too good for me," said Miss Miller, looking up from her book. "I was forced into playing with him, but no more!"

Luke pushed back his chair and swooped down

on Miss Miller. He tugged her book out of her hand and pulled her to her feet "You come stand beside me and give me moral support. I need you beside me always, Gwen."

Miss Miller suddenly stopped laughing. "Maybe Phyllis LaDere can help you. She couldn't keep away from you yesterday at the picnic."

"Jealous?" Luke tugged her hair. "I didn't think you cared."

Miss Miller lifted her chin. "You didn't?"

Libby didn't like Uncle Luke to tease Miss Miller.

Luke hugged Miss Miller. "You'd better care! I want you to. I'm beginning to think Scottie's idea the day he met you was a good one."

Miss Miller pulled free, her face red. "I'd better see if Mrs. Johnson needs any help."

Libby watched her hurry from the room, her skirt swishing around her slender legs. Uncle Luke had a very strange look on his face. Slowly he went over to sit across from Libby. Would Uncle Luke marry Miss Miller?

"Are you ready to finish?" he asked.

"Sure." Libby beat him without any trouble. She knew his mind wasn't on the game.

Just then Grandma walked in with Tammy LaDere beside her. Grandma rested her hand on Libby's shoulder. "Libby, Tammy wants you to walk downtown with her. And while you're there, pick up a small toy for Scottie. I promised him a surprise when he wakes up from his nap."

"Mother, are you spoiling my boy?" asked Luke sternly.

"Only a little," she answered, laughing. She looked so short beside him. "I haven't seen much of him these four years. I have to make up for it."

Luke slipped his arm around her waist. "I guess he needs a little spoiling from Grandma."

"Here's five dollars, Libby," said Grandma, holding out the folded money. "Buy yourself and Tammy a cola or something."

Libby slipped it into her pocket and reluctantly followed Tammy outdoors. The sun felt warm on her head. It was almost warm enough to wear a sun top and shorts.

"Are you still mad at me?" asked Tammy, lifting her purse strap to her shoulder.

"I guess not." Libby sighed. "I don't know why you wanted me to go shopping with you."

"Mom made me."

Libby gasped. Phyllis was using Tammy to check up on her!

"She said she'd buy me that gold chain I was looking at the other day. Remember?"

Libby nodded.

Tammy opened her purse and lifted out the gold chain. "But she won't have to buy that one. I took it this morning." She laughed. "Old Mr. Thompson kept looking at me, watching me, but I took it without him seeing me."

Libby's heart seemed to drop to her feet. Would the Johnsons have to know what her cousin was really like? It was very embarrassing.

Tammy fingered the chain. "I wish I'd had this to wear yesterday. I know Bob would have liked it." She sighed dreamily. "Someday I'm going to get married and have a house of my own." She looked at Libby. "Are you ever going to get married?"

"No." She intended to stay with the Johnsons forever.

"I let Bob kiss me yesterday. He didn't know how very well."

Libby stopped. "I don't want to walk with you if that's all you can talk about."

Tammy glared at her. "You're just jealous. You know no one will ever want to marry you!"

Libby stuck her face right up to Tammy's. "You won't get married, Tammy. You're just like your mother and my mother! And nobody will marry you!" Libby saw the fear, then anger in Tammy's eyes. Why had she said that to Tammy? She knew it would hurt her. Wouldn't she ever learn to keep her big mouth shut?

Tammy bumped against Libby roughly, almost knocking her into a store window. "I hate you, Libby! I won't talk to you again no matter what my mom wants!" She flipped her hair back, hoisted her purse strap to her shoulder, and rushed away.

Libby wanted to call after her and apologize, but her mouth seemed glued shut. She sighed unhappily. Slowly she walked into the store, the same store the gold chain came from. Too bad she'd said she would buy a toy for Scottie. How could she look at old Mr. Thompson knowing that Tammy had shoplifted the gold chain?

As Libby walked past the jewelry department she stared guiltily at the necklace tree. Did they know Tammy took a gold chain?

A strong hand clamped down on Libby's shoulder. She looked back into the angry face of old Mr. Thompson. She gasped.

"Young lady, I saw you slip a necklace into your purse this morning. I couldn't catch you then, but now I can. Give me the chain and don't ever come in here again."

Libby's heart raced. She opened her mouth, but no sound came out. Her throat seemed closed. Her mouth felt full of cotton. The man thought she was Tammy LaDere!

"I've wasted enough time with you. I'm calling your parents right now. What's the number? What's your name?"

"I . . . I didn't take anything. I really didn't!"

"I don't believe you. I've seen you in here often. And I've missed too many items. Turn out your pockets before I call the police to come do it." His mustache quivered as he talked. He towered over Libby. His deep voice grated against her ears.

She reached into her pockets. She knew she only had the five dollar bill that Grandma had given her. Something cold touched the fingers of her left hand. She lifted out the gold chain. Her heart stopped, then raced wildly. Tammy had slipped it in her pocket! But Mr. Thompson would never believe her.

He took a deep breath. She could tell he was having trouble controlling his anger. If he hit her, she'd sail across the store right through the window.

"So! You say you didn't take it! Honestly!" He grabbed the chain from her lifeless fingers. "You will not come in here again! I'll call your parents and then the police." He gripped her arm and tugged her toward the back of the store. "You sit right in there and stay put until I call your parents. Give me the number."

Libby told Grandpa's phone number in a voice that shook. Tears pricked her eyes as she huddled in the big chair near Mr. Thompson's desk.

"What's your name?" His eyes were full of hate as he looked at her over the telephone receiver.

"Libby," she whispered. "Please, please ask for Luke Johnson." She moistened her lips. "And tell him to bring Miss Miller."

The red phone looked small in the man's hand. His mustache brushed against the mouthpiece.

"Mr. Johnson, I have Libby here in my store. I caught her shoplifting. She says to bring Miss Miller when you come." He waited, listening. "I don't see why I should agree, but I won't call the police until I talk to you. Yes. Yes, I'm very sure I have the right girl. She had a gold chain in her pocket. I'm not mistaken."

Libby wanted to sink out of sight in the chair. Her chin rested on her thin chest. She closed her eyes tight. She would not cry!

Twelve
Albert

Libby pressed her cold hands against her hot cheeks. Would Uncle Luke believe her? Would Miss Miller?

Miss Miller's talk at the picnic flashed across Libby's mind. If God always knew who she was and where she was, then he knew what was happening to her now. God knew she hadn't taken the gold chain. He knew the trouble she was in.

Silently she asked her heavenly Father to get her out of trouble. She talked to him until Luke and Miss Miller walked in.

"Oh, Libby!" Miss Miller took Libby's cold hands. "What happened?"

She looked from Miss Miller's concerned face to Uncle Luke's stern face. Her mouth was dry and her throat ached. "I . . . I didn't do it," she whispered. Then she said firmly, "I didn't do it."

"Elizabeth!" Uncle Luke frowned at her. "The chain was in your pocket. Don't lie to us!"

"Luke!" said Miss Miller sharply. She held Libby close. "There has to be an explanation."

Libby pulled away from Miss Miller. "I didn't do it, Uncle Luke."

"I'll let it pass this time," said Mr. Thompson with a stern frown at Libby. "But I won't allow your girl in here again. She's been in several times the past few months. I suspected her of shoplifting, but I didn't catch her until this morning. I can't afford shoplifters!"

Luke stepped forward. "What are you saying? Libby has only been in town a few days. She wasn't out of the house this morning at all."

"I can trust my eyesight, young man!" Mr. Thompson chewed nervously on his mustache.

Miss Miller smiled reassuringly at Libby, then turned to Mr. Thompson. "I'm Libby's caseworker, Mr. Thompson. I keep a very close watch on her. She has been living about two hundred miles from here with this man's brother and his family. You have the wrong girl."

"Then it's her twin," snapped the man impatiently.

"Tammy LaDere!" exclaimed Luke. He drew the man aside and talked quietly with him. Libby watched, wishing she could hear what was being said.

"Everything's going to be all right, Libby," said Miss Miller softly. "I knew God would handle this, too."

Libby smiled as she blinked away tears. "I remembered to pray during my trouble for help out of it, Miss Miller. I thought of what you said at the picnic."

Miss Miller hugged her, then let her go. "I'm glad, Libby."

Luke walked to them, his face serious. "I want to call Phyllis right now and talk to her. I'm going to get her to bring Tammy here. Would you mind going out so I can talk privately?"

Miss Miller stiffened. "Not at all. Just keep in mind what she's really like."

Luke frowned. "We'll never agree on that, will we?" He turned away and walked to the phone.

Libby followed Miss Miller and Mr. Thompson from the office. Would Phyllis be angry at Luke? Would she convince him that Tammy hadn't shoplifted?

"Relax, Libby," said Miss Miller as they walked slowly down the aisle. "Luke will handle everything, I'm sure." But she didn't sound very sure. "Shall we choose a toy for Scottie while we wait?"

Libby nodded. She walked up and down the toy aisles. What would Scottie want most? What was Phyllis saying to Uncle Luke right now?

Miss Miller picked up a puzzle. "Would he like this?"

"It might be too hard for him." Libby rubbed the fur on a teddy bear. It looked like the baby to the bear she had at home on her bed. "He might like a stuffed animal."

Finally they decided on a red fire engine with detachable ladders. Libby paid at the counter, anxiously waiting for Uncle Luke. What was taking so long? She looked at Miss Miller. She was watching the office door very intently. Her knuckles were white from gripping her purse tightly.

The door burst open. Uncle Luke strode out, his face dark with anger. He stopped in front of Mr. Thompson. "You won't be bothered again. Tammy and her mother are leaving town." He dropped a twenty dollar bill on the counter. "I hope that covers some of your losses."

"It helps," said the man as he picked it up. He chewed nervously on his mustache. "I hope you won't hold it against me for accusing your girl falsely."

"We won't." Uncle Luke motioned for Miss Miller and Libby to follow him.

Libby clutched the bag with the fire engine and hurried out. Why was Uncle Luke so angry?

Miss Miller stopped beside Luke's car. "Will you please tell us what happened?"

"Not here. Not now. Get in the car." He jerked open the door, waited until Libby and Miss Miller climbed in, then slammed it shut. Libby watched as he strode around to his side.

"I'm scared," said Libby, shivering as she leaned against the front seat where Miss Miller sat.

"Don't be." Miss Miller reached around and patted her shoulder.

Luke slammed his door, then turned to Libby. "You are in big trouble, young lady! You have some explaining to do. We are going to a quiet spot where we can talk without interruption."

"What is it, Luke?" asked Miss Miller in concern.

Libby slumped against the back seat, her heart racing. She locked her fingers together until they hurt. It seemed to take an hour just to drive a short way into the country to a side road. She shivered as Uncle Luke turned off the key. He twisted around so he could talk.

"Don't be gruff, Luke. Be patient," said Miss Miller softly.

Libby stared at Luke, then dropped her eyes from the look in his.

"Why didn't you tell me they hated you, Libby? Do you know how much of a fool I feel?" Luke slapped his leg. "I was trying to help you, Libby. All the time I was making your life miserable!"

"What . . . what did Phyllis say?" asked Libby in a weak voice.

A car without a muffler roared past.

"At first she was sweetness and light, then when I told her that Tammy had taken the chain, not you, she called me every name in the book for believing you. She said a lot of ugly things about your mother, about you. I could not believe my ears." He looked at Miss Miller. "You were right. But if Libby had told me the truth, I would have believed it."

Miss Miller's face flamed. She turned quickly to stare out her window.

97

"I couldn't tell you, Uncle Luke!" cried Libby, scooting to the edge of the seat. "I just couldn't!"

"All right. All right. Calm down." He patted her hand that clutched the back of the seat. "She said some crazy thing about taking good care of Albert for you. Who's Albert?"

Libby moaned. The world seemed to spin about her.

Miss Miller turned in alarm. "Quick, Libby. Tell us!"

"Albert's Mrs. LaDere's cat," whispered Libby, her hazel eyes wide, her chest heaving. "Phyllis said if I told you anything, she'd kill Albert." Libby clutched Luke's hand that was resting on the back of the seat. "We've got to go right now! She's going to kill Albert! Maybe she already has!"

Luke turned sharply and started the car. He drove fast back to town and to the LaDeres. Libby could barely breathe. Miss Miller sat stiffly in the front seat.

The brakes squealed as Luke stopped outside the little white house. He leaped out and Libby followed.

Libby gasped. "Look! In the park!" She raced across to the park where old Mrs. LaDere sat huddled on a green park bench. Albert lay on her lap. Libby knelt in front of the woman. Finally she opened her eyes and looked into Libby's face. Tears streamed down her wrinkled cheeks.

"Albert's dead," she wailed. "He's dead!"

Luke sat beside her. Miss Miller stood beside Libby.

Libby pressed her hand against Albert. He was warm and limp. "He's not dead. We'll take him to the vet. He'll be all right. He has to be!"

Luke gathered the big cat in his arms. Libby and Miss Miller helped Mrs. LaDere to her feet. She stumbled but they supported her to the car.

Libby held Albert on her lap as Luke sped along. Libby remembered how she'd prayed for animals at the Johnson farm. She would pray for Albert. God had created animals, she reasoned, so he must love them. As she prayed she felt better. Would Mrs. LaDere want to know that she'd prayed for Albert?

"I heard a noise and I looked out the window," said Mrs. LaDere in between sobs. "I thought that terrible little dog was chasing Albert again. But he just flopped on the ground and didn't move. Phyllis and Tammy had left in a huff, so they couldn't help me with him."

"He'll be all right," said Miss Miller softly.

"He's all I have," said Mrs. LaDere, resting her hand on Albert's head. "He's all I've ever had."

Libby felt funny to hear her say that. Mrs. LaDere had Phyllis and Tammy and Marie Dobbs. Libby's heart lurched. And she had her, Libby. She was Mrs. LaDere's granddaughter. It felt strange to think that.

Libby sat close to Mrs. LaDere in the vet's waiting room. The chairs were scratched and scarred. A man holding a dog sat across the room from them. Miss Miller and Uncle Luke sat in a corner deep in conversation.

"Why are you being nice to me?" asked Mrs. LaDere sharply, looking at Libby with her watery blue eyes. "I don't have anything to give you."

"I want to help. I like Albert."

Mrs. LaDere nodded. "That's funny. He likes you, too. That's very strange."

Quietly Libby told about doctoring Snowball and Chester the calf and several of the other animals on the Johnson farm. "I like all of them. Most of them. They have a big white goose named Goosy Poosy. He knocked me down and I thought he was going to peck out my eyes." Libby looked quickly to see if the veterinarian was coming. He wasn't, so she continued talking. Mrs. LaDere was actually listening, forgetting for a time about her fear for Albert's life.

When he walked in he had Albert in his arms. Albert was alive, his eyes blinking. "Just keep him quiet a few days. Somebody must have hit him on the head pretty hard."

Mrs. LaDere hugged Albert close, baby-talking to him.

Libby looked quickly at Uncle Luke and Miss Miller. Should she tell Mrs. LaDere that Phyllis had probably hit the cat? She saw Miss Miller shake her head slightly as if to say not to tell.

Luke paid the bill, then ushered them all to his car. Libby tried to thank him, but he said it was nothing.

Miss Miller sat in the back with Libby while Mrs. LaDere sat in front, Albert safely on her lap.

"I can't pay you for this," she said sharply. "You'd better not expect me to."

"You don't have to pay me," he said kindly. "I did this for Libby. You have a wonderful granddaughter."

Mrs. LaDere sniffed disdainfully. Libby grinned with pride.

Miss Miller squeezed Libby's hand. "I think now you can enjoy the rest of your visit."

Libby leaned back with a sigh. "I think so too."

Thirteen
Grandpa's talk

Libby tightened her hold on her cup of cocoa as she stared across the kitchen table at Grandpa. "How can I do what you say?" she cried, her eyes wide. "I just can't!" She was glad the others were in the living room and that Scottie was already in bed for the night. She didn't want anyone to hear what Grandpa was saying to her.

He rubbed his graying hair back, then rested his hands on the table, his fingers locked together. "It's for your own good, Elizabeth. Do you know what happens to your spirit if you refuse to forgive?"

She shook her head, for the minute not caring at all.

"Listen to me, Elizabeth." Grandpa leaned toward her, his face serious. "Your spirit is to have clear communication to God. If you allow any sin to stay, you're blocking the lines of communication. God's Word says we must forgive others. It doesn't say if we feel like it or if the wrong done to us was only slight. But Jesus says we must forgive just as he forgives us." Grandpa reached across and took one of Libby's hands in his. "Honey, Phyllis and Tammy LaDere are not hurting because you won't forgive what they did to you and to Albert. But *you* are hurting. Even though you can't forgive them face to face, you can say inside yourself that you forgive every bad thing they did to you. Can you understand what I'm saying?"

"I think so." But she didn't want to!

"The wonderful thing about God is that he will help you forgive. He wants your spirit to be free. And I know that's what you want, too, Elizabeth. You value your relationship with your heavenly Father."

Libby looked at her hand in Grandpa's. She knew he was talking to her because he loved her. Yet he didn't love her nearly as much as God did. If God wanted her to forgive, then she'd do it. She looked up at Grandpa. "I do forgive them, Grandpa. I forgive them and I. . . ." She stopped. She'd almost said that she loved them. Oh, but she couldn't do that! She thought of Brenda Wilkens at home. She had thought she could never love Brenda either, but God had miraculously placed his love for Brenda in Libby's heart. He would have to do that again. She knew she couldn't love any of the LaDeres unless God loved them through her.

"Let's pray together, shall we, Elizabeth?" asked Grandpa as he walked around the table to stand beside Libby. When she nodded, he pulled her close and together they prayed.

And God worked a miracle. Suddenly Libby could understand why the LaDeres acted the way they did. They had no love for each other or for anyone else. What they needed was God's love, and to know they were loved by God. Libby prayed that God would send someone to them to show them God's love.

Several minutes later Grandpa and Libby walked happily into the living room. Grandma was asleep in her chair. Luke and Miss Miller sat on the couch, holding hands.

Luke looked up with a smile. "I'm trying to convince Gwen to marry me."

She blushed and tried to pull her hand free.

Grandpa chuckled. "I thought something was up." He sat down in his black leather chair and Libby sat on the floor beside him, her head on his leg. "I kind of think it's a little soon to talk marriage, isn't it, Luke? You two only met a few days ago."

Luke grinned. "No, Dad. We met over five years ago. We were going to get married then, but we had a little misunderstanding."

"Little!" Grandpa raised his eyebrows. "I'd say a big one since you married someone else."

Libby pulled her knees up under her chin and wrapped her arms around her legs. Miss Miller looked very uncomfortable. Was Uncle Luke teasing again?

"But Gwen waited all these years for me."
Luke frowned as Miss Miller jerked her hand
free. "Hey, I was only teasing."

Miss Miller leaped up, her cheeks flaming.
"He wanted to marry me then to make me
become a Christian. He wants to marry me now
to give his son a mother. Neither reason is good
enough for me!" She ran from the room but not
before Libby saw the tears in her eyes.

"What happened, Luke?" asked Grandma,
sitting up suddenly. "Why was Gwen so upset?"

Luke started for the door, then stopped.
"What's the use? She won't listen."

Libby didn't know if she should feel bad for
Miss Miller or for Uncle Luke. Or maybe for
Scottie. He wanted a new mother so badly. It
looked like Miss Miller didn't want that job.

"Sit down, son," said Grandpa kindly. "I've
had one good talk tonight. Maybe I can have
another with you." He squeezed Libby's
shoulder. "Libby and I talked and prayed
together. Now, son, maybe it's time you and I
did."

Libby squirmed uncomfortably. Should she
leave?

Luke sat on the couch, his head in his hands,
his elbows on his legs. His light blue shirt
stretched tightly across his wide shoulders. His
brown hair was mussed. "When will I learn?
That woman is so stubborn, so. . . ."

"And you love her," said Grandma softly.

Luke leaped to his feet. "Yes! Yes, I do! But she won't believe that. She wouldn't believe it before and she won't believe it now."

Libby moved closer to Grandpa.

"I'll admit I handled the whole thing wrong five years ago. She wasn't a Christian and I told her I wouldn't marry her because of that. Then I said I would marry her so I could teach her about Christ." He paced the room in agitation. "My words came out all wrong." He looked at Grandpa. "And they still come out wrong!"

"Sit down, son," said Grandpa. "I want you to remember that you are a child of the King." He waited until Luke was seated. "Any problem that you have concerns God. He wants to help you with every part of your life."

Libby listened as Grandpa talked. At times Grandma talked. Luke grew calm. Finally he asked if they could pray together.

Libby felt warm all over as they took her hand and included her in the prayer circle. Tears stung her eyes as Grandpa talked to God. What would her life with Marie Dobbs have been if they'd known how to talk to God?

Later Libby walked quietly upstairs to bed. She stopped outside Miss Miller's door. Should she go in and talk to her? Libby lifted her fist to knock. She leaned her head close. Miss Miller was sobbing. Slowly Libby turned away and walked to her room. Miss Miller would not want her to know she'd been crying. Libby would talk to her in the morning.

In her room Libby picked up the piano Joe had given her. Did she ever want to grow up and have adult problems? She touched the keys, longing to be able to sit at the piano at home and play until she couldn't think of anything except the melody.

The next morning she walked downstairs, tired from tossing and turning for so long the night before. She stopped, her hand gripping the banister. Miss Miller stood beside the front door, her suitcases at her feet.

"Where are you going?" whispered Libby.

Miss Miller jumped, then slowly turned. Her face was drawn and tired and she had dark circles under her eyes. "Home."

Libby hurried to her side. "But what about me?"

"Your Uncle Luke will take you home Saturday." Miss Miller buttoned her coat.

Libby clutched her arm. "I want to go with you! Don't leave me here!" Libby felt cold and unwanted. "Please, take me with you."

Miss Miller sighed. "All right, Libby. Your grandparents will be disappointed, but I'm sure they'll understand." She slipped off her coat and draped it over her largest suitcase. "I'll help you pack."

Libby looked up at a sound at the door. Grandma stood there with tears in her eyes.

"Oh, Libby, are you sure you want to go home today? Luke will take you Saturday. You'll enjoy riding with Scottie."

Libby rubbed her hands down her jeans. "I want to go with Miss Miller. Don't feel bad, Grandma."

She sighed. "OK, honey. I have breakfast ready for you. Come and eat first."

Libby took as much time getting ready as she could. Grandma had said that Uncle Luke, Grandpa, and Scottie had gone fishing. She wanted to give them a chance to get back before she left. Maybe Luke could stop Miss Miller from leaving before vacation time was over. Miss Miller kept urging Libby to hurry. Each minute she grew more nervous.

"Your car shouldn't give you any trouble going home," said Grandma as she stood beside the driver's window to talk to Miss Miller. "Luke said it was as good as new. But do drive carefully. I'll call Vera and Chuck later to let them know you're coming." She lifted her hand. "Bye, Libby. Bye, Gwen. Come again, please."

"Bye, Grandma," said Libby. Grandma looked so lonely standing in the yard all alone. Libby wished the others would hurry and get home from fishing. Why didn't Uncle Luke get back and stop Miss Miller? What could she do to keep Miss Miller in town a little longer? She twisted in her seat.

"I'd like to stop to see how Albert is today. Could we, please?" She held her breath.

Miss Miller hesitated. "All right, Libby. But don't stay long. I'd like to get home by noon."

Miss Miller stayed in the car as Libby ran to the door of the little white house across from the park. She knocked. Mrs. LaDere opened the door, then scowled.

"What do you want?" She clutched at her sweater.

"How's Albert today? I'm on my way home and I wanted to see him before I left."

Reluctantly Mrs. LaDere opened the door wide and allowed Libby to walk in. "Don't disturb Albert. He's taking a nap. Just look at him, then get out."

Libby looked at her grandmother sadly. What a difference between Grandma Johnson and this woman!

Albert opened his eyes and lifted his head. Libby knelt beside his bed and gently stroked him. "I'm glad you're well, Albert. I prayed for you."

"That's a dumb thing to say," snapped Mrs. LaDere with a scowl. "Nobody prays for a cat."

Libby stood up. "I do. You see, I know that God loves me. He cares for the animals we love, too. I didn't want Albert to die, so I prayed." Libby touched Mrs. LaDere's thin arm. "God loves you."

She brushed Libby's hand away. "Silly nonsense. Your time is up. I don't want you bothering to come again." She jerked open the door and waited until Libby walked out.

Libby climbed into the car and slumped

against the seat. How could her own grandma be so mean?

"What's wrong, Libby?" asked Miss Miller.

"Let's just get out of here," snapped Libby. "I don't care if I never come back."

Fourteen
Home again

The only noise in the car as they drove along was a fly buzzing against Miss Miller's window. Impatiently she rolled it down. The wind carried the fly out.

Libby had tried not to think about Mrs. LaDere, but she couldn't keep the thoughts from coming. Grandpa had said she was to forgive and love. How could she love someone who didn't want love? But she knew the answer. She couldn't forgive, or love, unless she asked Jesus to help her. She thought of how she and Grandpa had prayed, then again of them praying for Luke and Miss Miller. Grandma had said God could handle any problem, any situation.

"You're very quiet, Libby," said Miss Miller stiffly.

"So are you."

"Was Mrs. LaDere sharp with you?"

"Yes! She doesn't want anything to do with

me." Libby turned to Miss Miller. "Can she be happy with just Albert?"

"No, Libby. Albert does help take away some of the loneliness. But she can't be happy. She needs you, Libby. She needs you to show you care, that you're thinking about her. I saw her come to the door as if she was going to call you back, then she closed it again."

Libby thought about that a long time. She looked at Miss Miller. A tear stood on her cheek. "Are you mad at Uncle Luke?"

Miss Miller was taken aback. She looked pained.

"He wants to marry you and you're going home," Libby continued.

"I don't want to talk about it, Libby."

"Luke talked to us about it last night. We prayed."

"Oh," Miss Miller said in a tiny voice.

"I don't want you to be mad at him."

"I'd rather not discuss it, Libby!" She kept her eyes glued to the road.

Libby stared out her window. The countryside flashed past. Soon they'd be near the city, away from fresh air and farmland. Once they drove through the city they'd be close to the Johnson farm. It would be wonderful to be home again! She thought about Joe and the tiny piano he'd given her. She gasped. She hadn't packed the piano.

"Miss Miller!" she cried. "Did you pack that tiny piano that was on the dresser in my room?"

She frowned. "Was that yours? I left it there."

"Oh, no! How can I get it back?"

Miss Miller patted her arm. "Luke is coming down Saturday. Just call and ask him if he'll bring it."

Libby sighed in relief. "Will you talk to him when he comes?"

"No. I'll be very busy this weekend getting ready to go back to work." She slipped in a tape. Music filled the car. Libby knew that meant not to talk about anything.

Goosy Poosy waddled across the driveway as they drove in. Miss Miller had to slow down until he was safely in the grass. Libby was so glad to be home that she almost felt like hugging Goosy Poosy.

As the car stopped, the front door opened and Vera rushed out. Libby leaped out of the car and into Vera's arms. She smelled as if she'd been frying chicken.

"It's so good to have you home!" said Vera against Libby's hair. "I missed you very much."

"I missed you, too." Libby pulled away as Miss Miller set her suitcase on the ground beside her.

"Will you come in for a while, Gwen?" asked Vera with a smile. "I'm sure you're tired after driving so far."

"I really must hurry home." Miss Miller smiled weakly. "I'll come out some time when I can stay a while and chat. Goodbye, Libby."

"Bye," mumbled Libby. She wanted to say a

lot of things, but she didn't want to upset Miss Miller and make her cry again.

"Thank you for taking Libby to visit and bringing her home again," said Vera. They stood there until Miss Miller drove out of the driveway toward town. "Well, Libby, Grandma tells me you met several new relatives. Let's go inside and talk before the gang gets home from school."

Libby shivered. She didn't know if she wanted to tell Vera about her real relatives. She wanted to talk about Luke and Scottie and what to do for Miss Miller.

Vera had a fire burning in the fireplace in the family room. Libby sat beside it near Vera's feet. Libby talked until her mouth was dry. Once she started telling how she felt and what had happened to her, she couldn't stop. Several times Vera brushed tears from her eyes.

Finally Libby jumped up. "I have to go see Snowball. Did Toby learn to ride Dusty by himself yet? Did Susan remember to feed that little calf?"

Vera laughed and tugged Libby's hair playfully. "The place did not fall apart just because you were gone. Toby did learn to ride. He fell off twice but only got dirty."

Libby slipped on her barn coat and ran to the barn. Goosy Poosy honked wildly and flew after her, wings flapping and neck out. Libby stepped inside the barn and hastily closed the door. Goosy Poosy honked, then finally walked away. A barn cat rubbed against Libby's leg. She leaned down and picked him up, stroking him and talking to him.

In Snowball's stall she stood a long time just hugging the white filly. Oh, it had been so long!

Just as she finished saying hello to all the animals, the school bus stopped at the end of the driveway. Shouts and laughter filled the air, then she heard the bus starting up again to go let off Brenda and Joe Wilkens.

Libby shouted and waved as she dashed down the driveway toward Ben, Susan, Kevin, and Toby.

"You're back! You're back!" cried Susan, hugging Libby tightly. "We didn't think you'd be here before Saturday. I'm so glad you came back early."

Libby hugged the others. She was so happy she thought she would pop right open. She thought of her real family and her smile vanished for a moment. How thankful she was that the Johnsons had prayed her into their family!

Everyone talked at once, trying to tell Libby all they'd done while she was gone. They talked while they did outside chores. They talked while they did inside chores. Libby wanted to listen and listen. She would never, never go away again unless all of them went with her.

"Here comes Dad," said Kevin breathlessly. "Quick, let's hide Libby and surprise him." Kevin punched his glasses on his nose. His blond hair stood on end. "Stand behind Dad's plaid coat. We'll stand in front of you."

Libby almost smothered under the coat. She waited, then heard the kids say, "Hi, Dad. Did you have a good day today?"

"This is some greeting," said Chuck, laughing. "What surprise do you have for me?"

"What do you mean?" asked Ben.

"Nobody meets me at the door unless something's up."

Libby wrinkled her nose. She knew she was going to sneeze.

"Surprise!" shouted Kevin, jerking aside the farm coat.

Libby saw the surprised look on Chuck's face, then he grabbed her and hugged her tightly.

"Elizabeth! I've missed you! I'm never letting you go away again, not even to my parents." He held her away from him, then hugged her again.

A noise at the back door made them all turn. Luke and Scottie stood there.

"Luke!" cried Chuck, grabbing his brother's hand, then hugging him. "Come in! Did you bring Elizabeth home? Is that why she's early?"

Libby took Scottie's hand and introduced him to Toby.

Suddenly Scottie turned and held his hand out to Libby. "I found it and I knew it was yours. So, I brought it."

Libby looked. It was her tiny piano that Joe had given her. She took it and held it to her, then hugged Scottie and told him thank you.

Finally when the noise was down and everyone was getting ready for supper, Luke walked up to Libby. "Where's Gwen?" he asked quietly. He looked tired and sad.

"She brought me here, then went home."

"How did she seem?"

"Sad."

Luke sighed unhappily. "I didn't think she'd run off without seeing me first. I tried to call her but there was no answer."

"She was crying." Libby felt like crying, too. She thought Uncle Luke was going to.

But suddenly he smiled. "Libby, my girl, I am not going to worry. This problem is in God's hands. He will help me find a way to convince Miss Gwen Miller that I love her and want to marry her."

Supper was a noisy, happy time. Vera had fried chicken as only she could fix it, along with creamy mashed potatoes, buttered corn, a tossed salad, and strawberry Jello with bananas for dessert.

Libby sat back with a satisfied smile. If Miss Miller would drive up now everything would be perfect. Libby leaned forward as a fantastic idea popped into her head. She'd call Miss Miller and tell her she needed her badly. Miss Miller would almost fly out. And she did need her badly for Uncle Luke's happiness.

Quietly Libby slipped to the study to use the phone. Her hand trembled as she dialed Miss Miller's number. Her voice shook as she told Miss Miller that she needed her right now, tonight.

"Libby, you sound terrible! What is it, honey? Can't you tell me now?"

"I'll tell you as soon as you get here. Please, please hurry!"

Libby smiled as she replaced the receiver. She looked around the quiet study where she'd had so many private conversations with Chuck and even with Miss Miller. This would be the perfect place for Uncle Luke and Miss Miller to talk.

But right now she'd have to tell Luke what she'd done. Her hazel eyes sparkled excitedly as she hurried to the family room.

Fifteen
Happy ever after

Libby stood outside the church, smiling
happily as Uncle Luke and her new Aunt Gwen
ran to the gaily decorated car. Shoes and tin cans
were tied on the back just below the JUST
MARRIED sign. Libby smoothed down her frilly
pink dress. It was sure different from her blue
jeans and sweat shirt!

"Isn't it romantic," Brenda Wilkens said to
Ben just in back of Libby. "They are so much in
love! Oh, Ben, I could watch them all day long."

Libby wanted to tell Brenda to shut up. But
today she wouldn't do anything to ruin anyone's
happiness. She waved at Miss Miller—no, Aunt
Gwen! She thought of the day two weeks ago
when she'd called for Miss Miller to come to see
her. She'd rushed in and Libby had walked to the
study, opened the door, then shut it behind her.
Libby had waited outside the study door. Miss
Miller had squealed, then all was quiet. Libby

119

knew Uncle Luke was taking care of everything. He'd convinced her to marry him. Scottie finally had his new mother.

Libby looked at Scottie standing between Chuck and Vera. He looked happy enough to fly. He was staying a week on the farm while Uncle Luke and Aunt Gwen went on their honeymoon.

"You look very pretty today, Elizabeth."

Libby turned at Grandpa's voice. "Thank you. I feel pretty too. My dress was almost as pretty as the bride's."

Slowly Libby walked with Grandpa across the parking lot of the church. Several people were leaving. The Bennetts drove past and Libby waved.

"I saw your Grandma LaDere two days ago, Elizabeth," said Grandpa as he stopped beside his car and leaned against it. "Albert was walking along beside her as if he owned the world."

"I'm glad he's all right." Libby stood away from the car so she wouldn't get her dress dirty.

"Mrs. LaDere looked tired and lonely. I stopped to talk to her a while. She was very surprised that I would." Grandpa jangled the keys in his pocket. "It made me realize what little I've actually done to help her. Grandma and I are going to do our best to become friends with her."

Libby shivered. She remembered the woman's sharp voice and angry manner. Nobody could make friends with her. Not even her own family.

"Have you written to her at all, Elizabeth?"

Libby looked up sharply. "No! She wouldn't want to hear from me."

"How do you know?"

"I just do." She looked at the toes of her white shoes. Mrs. LaDere would probably send a letter zipping right back unopened.

Grandpa tugged his tie loose. "It's harder to convince some people that you love them. Mrs. LaDere has been without love for so long that she forgot what it was like. She loves Albert. He won't do anything to hurt or embarrass her. And Albert won't leave her to make a life of his own." Grandpa chuckled. "That cat is smarter than some people I know."

Libby half listened as Grandpa changed the subject to fishing. She was thinking of Mrs. LaDere's lonely life. Had Phyllis and Tammy stayed away as they said they intended to do? Who would love Mrs. LaDere?

Libby shifted from one foot to the other. The sun felt hot against her head. She wanted to go home and take off her beautiful dress. She felt better in her jeans and sweat shirt.

Grandpa tapped her arm. "Go get Grandma and tell her I'm ready to go home. I want to rest a while." He opened the car door and climbed inside.

Libby hurried back to the church, her shoes tapping on the pavement. She met Brenda Wilkens just outside the door. She was alone. Libby's heart dropped to her feet. She tried to

121

walk past Brenda, but Brenda stood firmly in her way.

"I hear that even your own relatives don't want you, aid kid," said Brenda, looking down her nose at Libby.

Libby doubled up her firsts. Brenda was asking for another bloody nose.

"It must be hard not having anyone to love you, aid kid." Brenda flipped back her long black hair.

Libby smiled. It wasn't a forced smile. Jesus was helping her. "Brenda, nothing you can say to me will upset me. I know how important love is. I'm sorry that my real family doesn't know about love. Just maybe I can help them learn."

Brenda gasped. "Something is wrong with your head. How can *you* do anything for anybody?"

"I have to find Grandma, Brenda. Excuse me, please." And Brenda was so stunned that she stepped aside. Libby smiled as she went to find Grandma. Brenda's words rang in her head. "It must be hard not having anyone to love you." Was Mrs. LaDere finding it hard? Libby frowned thoughtfully. What could she do to help her find love? Maybe write a letter as Grandpa had suggested.

Libby stopped beside Grandma. She was laughing and talking freely to several women. Libby couldn't imagine Mrs. LaDere doing that. Grandma was full of love. She gave and received love.

"Where's Grandpa?" asked Grandma, looking at Libby.

"He's waiting for you in the car. He's tired and wants to go home now."

"I'm tired myself." She walked with Libby. "Luke was very happy today. Happier than I've ever seen him. When he kissed me goodbye he said to tell you thank you again for helping him with Gwen. They're going to be very happy, Libby."

"I'm glad!" Libby walked to the car with Grandma. Suddenly she wanted to go home too and take off her dress and put on her jeans. She wanted to pet Snowball and run with Rex. "Can I ride with you, Grandma?"

"Of course, honey. We'll just stop long enough to tell Vera or Chuck."

The inside of the car was cool and comfortable. Libby waved to Joe Wilkens as Grandpa called to tell Chuck that Libby was riding with them.

An hour later Libby sat cross-legged on her bed, the tiny grand piano in her hand. She was dressed in jeans and a yellow tee shirt. Gently she touched the keys. What would she play on it if it were real? Someday she'd sit at a real grand piano and play music to hundreds of people. Would Mrs. LaDere want to hear her play? Would she tell everyone around that the girl at the piano was her granddaughter? Libby sighed. Mrs. LaDere would stay at home with Albert on her lap. Year after year she'd sit in her little white house and nobody would care enough to bother with her.

A tear slipped down Libby's cheek and landed on the piano. Libby carefully rubbed it away. She looked slowly around her room. The red, dark pink, and pink were almost too beautiful for words. Someone who cared had decorated this room to show love. Vera had said that when she'd chosen the wallpaper, drapes, and bedspread, she'd asked the Lord to send them just the right girl.

"I'm that girl," whispered Libby. They had prayed her into this home, this family. Love had come into her life, and nothing was the same for her.

Chuck poked his head in the doorway, then walked in with a smile. "Here you are, Elizabeth. I was looking for you."

"Did you need me for something?"

He sat on the edge of the bed. "I was lonely for you."

Libby beamed. She knew just what he meant. Sometimes she'd get lonely for him, for Vera, for the kids in her new family.

"I can remember when Luke was just a little boy. I was almost ten when he was born. Time goes fast, Elizabeth. Never waste a minute of it! When I saw Luke today my mind flashed back to when he was born and it seemed like yesterday." Chuck rubbed his red hair off his wide forehead. "I looked around at you children and I knew that in a few years I'd see you grown and on your own. I love you, Elizabeth. I want you to know that now and I want you to remember that when you're grown."

Libby leaned forward and kissed Chuck. "I love you." She remembered when those words had been very hard to say. It had taken time to get them past her lips. They'd been in her heart, but she hadn't been able to say them. "I love you, Dad," she said again, just because it felt so good to say it. Would Mrs. LaDere ever learn to love?

Chuck touched the piano in Libby's hand. "That is a gift to treasure always. Joe could have given you something that was important to him, but he chose something that was important to you."

They talked for a long time. When Chuck walked out, Libby sat very still and just looked at her piano. She could look at that and know that Joe liked her. It made her feel good. Was there some way that she could show Mrs. LaDere that she was important? That she was loved?

Slowly Libby climbed off her bed. She walked to her desk and sat down. The puzzle box from her real dad sat beside a tablet of paper. She rubbed the shiny surface of the puzzle box. It had been full of secrets to help her learn to know and love her real dad.

Libby picked up the tablet. Could she write to Mrs. LaDere once a week and slowly show that she loved her? Libby gasped. She did love her! And she wasn't loving her on her own. Jesus had placed the love in her heart. "Thank you, Jesus," whispered Libby.

She opened her desk drawer and pulled out a ball point pen. She poised it over the lined paper.

"Dear Mrs. LaDere," she wrote. She looked at it. That wouldn't do at all. She tore off the sheet, balled it up, and tossed it into her wastebasket.

"Dear Grandma LaDere," she said as she wrote it at the top of the paper. Libby tipped her head and studied the words. They looked just right.

"Today Uncle Luke and Gwen Miller were married." Libby chewed on the end of the pen as she thought. "I wore a new dress."

Libby wrote and wrote until her hand grew tired and cramped. She felt like singing. She would share herself, her love, with Grandma LaDere. Then she would have more than just Albert. Someday she'd learn to love as Libby had learned.

With a flourish Libby signed the letter, "Your granddaughter, Libby." "I love you, Grandma LaDere," she whispered. "And someday you'll believe me."

Libby jumped to her feet. Suddenly she had to see her family. She could hear them talking in the family room as she dashed downstairs. It was time to sit with them, talk to them, love them. Oh, it was so good to be loved!